Death By Haunting
A Josiah Reynolds Mystery

Abigail Keam

Worker Bee Press

The history is true. The art thefts are true.
The artists are real, but the art may not be.
The characters are not based on you.
So don't go around town and brag about it.
Josiah Reynolds does not exist except in the author's mind.

ISBN 978 0 9906782 0 5

8 12 15

Published in the USA by

Worker Bee Press
P.O. Box 485
Nicholasville, KY 40340

Abigail Keam

Acknowledgements

Thanks to my editor, Patti DeYoung.

Special thanks to Sarah Moore
for her insight.

Artwork by Cricket Press
www.cricket-press.com

Book jacket by Peter Keam
Author's photograph by Peter Keam

To Susie, Debbie, Paul, and Mike

By The Same Author

Death By A HoneyBee I
Death By Drowning II
Death By Bridle III
Death By Bourbon IV
Death By Lotto V
Death By Chocolate VI
Death By Haunting VII
Death By Derby VIII

The Princess Maura Fantasy Series

Wall Of Doom I
Wall Of Peril II
Wall Of Glory III
Wall Of Conquest IV
Wall of Victory V

Last Chance For Love Romance Series

Last Chance Motel I
Gasping For Air II
The Siren's Call III

Short Stories

Bobby Bobo Got Baptized At The Big Bone Baptist Church

Audio Books

Prologue

Mr. Bailey, who lived up Tates Creek Road from Josiah Reynolds, was awakened in the wee hours of the night to find that his covers had been pulled off. His growling Jack Russell terrier and clinging orange tabby were lying so close to him as to be almost pushing Mr. Bailey off his new mattress.

"What the . . .?" muttered Mr. Bailey, as he turned to push the cat away and question his wife of forty-seven years. "Mavis! What's going on?" asked Mr. Bailey, as he turned on his side to find his missus wide-eyed and sitting straight up against the headboard of their new poster bed, staring into a darkened corner of their bedroom.

Mavis pointed toward the corner and croaked, "Mama's here."

Mr. Bailey followed his wife's outstretched hand pointing to a dark corner where indeed stood his mother-in-law, Cordelia Sharp, wearing her favorite blue seersucker summer dress and lavender wig.

The only problem was that Cordelia Sharp had been dead for seven years.

1

My name is Josiah Reynolds. I was named for the Hebrew king in the Old Testament.

Old King Josiah purified the Temple from idolatry and cult prostitution. He ordered that all the priests who followed the pagan gods and goddesses be killed.

To be sure, it was the King's way or the highway, buddy, for if his soldiers caught up with you, it meant an unpleasant death.

I am a widow-woman and until recently was the object of an extreme stalker who ended up falling over the Cumberland Falls and crashing on the rocks below. But not before the creep had shot my dog and two of my friends, one of whom is still fighting for his life.

But going over the Falls is not how he died. Someone put a bullet through his chest as he was trying to drown me in the Cumberland River.

I don't know who killed my nemesis, O'nan, and I really don't give a rat's . . . well, you know. I'm just glad he's dead.

My daughter swore on the Bible it was not she. I made her put her hand on the Good Book and swear an oath to me. I hope Asa is Southern enough to believe that if she lied, she will be cursed. But that doesn't mean she couldn't have had someone else do it for her.

I have a few other names in the hat, but I really don't care except that I am left with the repercussions of O'nan's actions. And the repercussions are painful.

2

It was one of the most difficult decisions I had ever had to make, but I thought it the right one. I just have to tell Franklin. He would have a fit and there was a strong possibility he might never forgive me, but it had to be done. I would tell him later as I had to stop by the Big House first since I had gotten a call from my next-door neighbor, Lady Elsmere.

Lady Elsmere, aka June Webster from Monkey's Eyebrow, Kentucky, had the penchant for marrying wealthy men who died at an early age. Widowed twice, she was as rich as Midas and had come back to her Kentucky roots after living in England for several decades. She had been my friend for many years and she helped my deceased husband with his career by letting him restore her antebellum home, which is still a showstopper in the Bluegrass.

I call her home the Big House. Both Lady Elsmere and I like to pretend that we live in a Tennessee Williams' play. Very often, we are not wrong.

After pushing in the code for the massive steel front gate, I drove up the pin oak-lined driveway and parked in the back of the house so I could go into the servants' entrance where there were no steps.

I no longer relied on my cane, but why tempt fate? You see, I had had a terrible fall. I fell off an eighty-foot cliff crashing into a ledge midway down. The fall busted my face, most of my teeth, lots of bones, and my pride. As a result, I limp, wear a hearing aid, and pee on myself every time I burp.

On the positive side, I am no longer fat and when they were reconstructing my face, the docs gave me a little helpful boost in the age department. I look younger than I am, and my new teeth are so bright, they positively glow in the dark. I never need a flashlight anymore. I just smile.

To tell you the truth, I am held together with spit and a prayer.

I tried the door. Of course, it was unlocked.

When would June realize that she and her staff could no longer live like it was 1959 when no one in Lexington locked their doors?

I entered through the mudroom, sat on a bench and took off my snow boots, putting on the slippers I had brought with me.

We had recently had a late snowstorm just when the fruit trees were blooming. Weather in Kentucky can be freakish at times as winter yields to spring begrudgingly.

While I was hanging up my coat, Bess poked her head in and said, "Just wanted to see who came a'callin'."

"Bess, you really need to start locking the doors. Anyone could have come in."

"You're so right. So right. There's a lot of meanness in the world."

"You're not gonna start locking the back door, are you?" I complained, giving a look of consternation and following her into the kitchen.

Bess laughed while beating egg whites into a meringue. "Nope. Tired of living in fear. O'nan is dead and like the Israelites, we are set free."

"There are other bad people out there, Bess," I said, giving her a big hug from behind. "Remember that boy who tried to steal your Christmas jewels?"

"Get off with you," laughed Bess. "Can't you see that I'm in the middle of making a masterpiece here?"

"Where's Charles and your mama?"

"Mummy went to Charleston to see her people and you know, where Mummy goes, so does Daddy. She wanted to show off her new jewelry that June gave her for Christmas."

"Who's doing the butler stuff?"

"Liam." Bess spooned the stiff whites on the chocolate pies. "He's not half bad . . . when he's not under the weather."

"Is that what we are calling him now?" I asked, as Liam had been known as Giles until recently.

It seems that Liam Doyle had been a thief by profession in another life and the Irishman had been hiding from the police under the disguise of an English valet. I guess his past had been ironed out as he was using his real name and that Lady Elsmere had decided to keep him. I know it's hard to keep up with all of this.

Bess nodded while beating more egg whites.

I waited for her to say more about Giles, I mean, Liam, but she was silent. Darn! I continued, "That's good. Maybe Charles and your mother can retire then."

"June said . . . I mean Lady Elsmere," teased Bess, giving a wicked grin, "that Daddy can't retire from the Big House until she's dead and buried in the ground."

"That may not be for some time."

Bess torched the meringue with a kitchen blowtorch, darkening the edges. "She'll outlive us all. She's having too much fun to die."

"I know that things have been tried in the past to help lessen the strain on your daddy."

"Part of the problem is that Daddy misses the house when he's not in charge and thinks no one can do as good a job."

"And he is right. No one takes care of this house like Charles but he's got to oversee the farm, take care of June's charities plus he's on the board of the Humane

Society. That's way too much for anybody. June can't live forever."

"Who says I can't?" demanded June, walking into the massive kitchen. "Are you trying to shove me into the grave, naughty girl?"

"NOOOO. We were just talking about how you make Charles' life miserable."

"Pshaww. Charles lives to complain. It's one of his endearing qualities. Right, Bess?"

Shaking her head, Bess turned to study her pies. "If you say so, Miss June, but Daddy's not getting any younger."

"I do say so," Miss June replied, giving me a long sideways glance. "Now what do you want? I just loaned Miss Eunice my best silver for some wedding reception you're having at your place. Have you come to collect it?"

"If you get one of the boys to put it in my car, I'll take it. However, you called me—remember?"

June started down the hallway. "What terrible weather to have a wedding reception. Just think of it. Supposed to be in the seventies next week. I guess the tornadoes will follow. They love to come with the spring rainstorms."

"June, what are you rattling on about?"

"The weather. Everyone talks about the weather. Ahem."

I looked up and saw that June was standing in front of a newly acquired painting hanging in the hallway by the grand staircase.

On the wall was an oil painting of eight riders on horses racing beneath a dramatic stormy sky. It was gorgeous.

I leaned toward it. Were the horses in a race or were the riders exercising the horses and racing against the storm to get back to the barn? No, they had to be in a race as the riders were wearing silks. Looking for the name, I spied the "John Hancock" of John Henry Rouson.

"John Henry Rouson," I mumbled out loud. "Never heard of him."

"Oh my dear, he is very famous . . . or was. Lord Elsmere actually introduced us in England."

"I'm not much into equine art."

"Living in Kentucky and you don't know who the famous horse painters are? I can't believe that I have found a topic that I know more about than you." June tapped her foot. "Well, what do you think of it?"

"I think it's gorgeous. Where did you get it?"

"From Jean Louis. He brought his entire collection with him to Kentucky while he's working on my portrait. He said he couldn't bear not to see them for even one day. Isn't that quaint?"

"Suspicious is what I call it. If he can't part with them, why did he give you one?"

"Oh, don't be such a gloomy cuss. Not everyone is on the make."

"How much did you pay for it?"

"It was a gift. See there!"

I gave the painting a curious look.

Lady Elsmere continued, "He saw me admiring it and just gave it to me. Come. Come. You must see my new portrait. Of course, it's not done . . . just the bones . . . but it's wonderful. So like me."

I followed June down the hallway to the library. She opened the door.

Inside I smelled oil paint, turpentine, and the raw material of canvas. There were tarps thrown on the antique parquet floor in order to accommodate the huge wooden easel holding a very large canvas.

Behind the easel was Jean Louis puttering. He poked his head around. "Ah, bonjour mes amies." He waved us in. "Entrez s'il vous plait. I was just cleaning my brushes."

"I hope we're not intruding," said June.

"Lady Elsmere, you are never a bother. I see you bring the beautiful Josiah with you. Please come in. Madame Josiah, you have not come to visit me lately. Makes me think you don't like me. Oui?"

"I've been busy with a sick friend."

"Yes. Yes. It happened right after I arrived. Your friend, Monsieur Mathew Garth. He was shot, no?"

"Yes, and he is still gravely ill."

Jean Louis pursed his lips. "So sad when someone is so young."

"Yes, very sad for everyone."

"But the bad man is dead, n'est-ce pas?"

"So they tell me," I replied. I didn't like to talk about O'nan. He was a rogue cop who had stalked me for several years, making my life a living hell.

"But I forget my manners. Please sit. Lady Elsmere, might we have tea?"

"Of course. Please pull that rope for the butler."

"I'll take care of it," I announced, opening the library door. I poked my head out into the hallway and yelled, "Hey Bess, can we have some tea?"

"Yeah, give me a minute or two," she yelled back.

"Okay." I closed the door. "It will be a minute or two," I deadpanned. Yes, I did that just to be a stinker.

Lady Elsmere squinted at me with fury while Jean Louis twiddled with his mustache, looking amused.

I smiled sweetly and sat down on a couch in front of the portrait.

I hated when Lady Elsmere put on airs. After all, she was just June Webster from Monkey's Eyebrow, Kentucky, and was raised on a farm shoveling horse manure like most of her generation. The only reason she had money was that her first husband was a genius and had invented some doohickey in his garage that made them both rich. He died of a heart attack while they were touring Europe and she then married Lord Elsmere, who was in need of a Lady but didn't necessarily "need" a lady, if you know what I mean.

"So this is the painting," I drawled without enthusiasm. "She already has two. The head and shoulders over the fireplace in her bedroom and the full-length portrait in the dining room."

"Yes, but this is one of a woman in the full bloom of her maturity," replied Jean Louis.

"You mean ancient," I quipped.

"Really, Josiah, I don't see why you are being so unpleasant this afternoon. If I want another portrait, what business is that of yours?"

I felt the heat rise to my cheeks. I *was* being awful. "I'm sorry, June. My apologies, Jean Louis. I just had to make a difficult decision and I'm afraid that I am taking it out on the both of you. I'm so sorry. Really, I am."

June gasped, "You didn't pull the plug on Matt, did you?"

"Of course not."

"Oh, goodness. Just for a moment I thought you had —well, you know."

"Matt is doing better, but recuperation is going to take longer than expected. The bullet ricocheted in his body, hitting some vital organs." I threw my hands up and stammered, "I . . . I hate to even talk about it. Again, my apologies for being a tyrant."

"It is reasonable, Madame, that you wish to express your anger at the injustice of the situation in which you find yourself. However, maybe Lady Elsmere and I can take your mind off your difficulty at least for a few minutes."

June sat beside me and patted my hand. "Jean Louis is right. Let's talk about something else for awhile."

I smiled kindly at June.

She clapped her wrinkled hands. "Let's talk about my portrait. What do you think?"

Wearily I finally focused on the life-sized portrait of June complete with tiara, diamond necklace, bracelet, and rings. I had to admit it was stunning and June looked rather majestic.

The background was very dark, which emphasized the shimmering yellow organza ball gown that June wore, sitting with her hands folded on her lap. While her face portrayed serene countenance, it was her eyes that caught the viewer's interest. They seemed so animated that one might say a fire was emanating from them.

"Ummm. You look rather regal."

"Really? So you like it?" asked June.

"Now where is this painting going?"

"After my death, the University of Kentucky Medical Center will receive a large endowment and this portrait as well."

"So it is going to be hung in public then." I stared at the portrait, not knowing how to say it. Surely she must know.

"June, I think it's lovely, but don't you think it looks quite similar to the 1954 portrait of Queen Elizabeth by Sir William Dargie? You know, the one where she is wearing a yellow gown and now hangs in the Australian Parliament. I mean . . . except for the face, they are almost identical."

"Oh, Lizzie won't mind."

"Lizzie? You call the Queen 'Lizzie'? I didn't know that was a pet name for Her Majesty."

At that moment the door opened and in weaved Liam carrying a tea tray. "Shall I pour, Madam?" asked Liam.

"No thank you. Josiah can do that."

I made a face, as I disliked being conscripted to perform such tasks. The strength in my hands sometimes gave out without notice, causing me to drop things.

Seeing my discomfort, Jean Louis spoke up. "Put it by me, Liam. I'll pour for the ladies."

"Very good, Sir." Liam put the tea tray on a small table near us and left quickly, but not before I caught a whiff of whisky on him.

I stood up. "You must excuse me. It has been a long day and I'm very tired. Shall we do this another time?"

"Naturellement," replied Jean Louis, fluttering his pudgy hands.

"I'll walk you out," suggested June, giving me a concerned look. "You do look tired, Josiah."

"You stay and enjoy your tea. My car is out back. No need for you to walk all that distance."

"All right, but don't forget that I will pick you up tomorrow morning at ten thirty sharp."

I gave a blank look.

"For Terrence Bailey's memorial."

"Oh dear, I forgot. I promised Eunice that I would help her with the reception."

"I'll send Bess over to help Eunice. You go with me. Mavis would consider it a slight if we didn't show up, being neighbors and all."

"Won't she consider it a slight if Bess doesn't come?"

"Naw, she never liked Bess. Something about an ingredient being left out of a recipe that Bess was supposed to have given her years ago."

"Okay, I'll be ready, but I can't stay forever. I must be home by one."

June looked disappointed. She loved a good funeral and usually was the last to leave the wake. I think it was because she had a fondness for Jell-O desserts. At least one person usually brought Jell-O, especially if that person was over the age of sixty.

I gave a goodbye nod to Jean Louis and made my way out of the Big House, but not before Bess gave me one of her chocolate pies.

Gratefully, I accepted it. I was going to use it as a peace offering to Eunice when I told her I was going to a funeral in the morning instead of helping her.

I just hoped the pie was not going to be thrown back in my face.

3

Since I didn't have the stamina to stand in long lines and June teetered as though she were going to fall over any moment, we both sat until the receiving line had thinned out.

The memorial had turned out to be a visitation. The funeral was the next day. I felt stupid sitting all dressed up in my widow's weeds, but June loved the drama of it all.

Seeing that Mavis was getting tired of standing too, her daughter deposited her next to us. "Josiah, can you keep an eye on Mama for me?" she asked before joining her husband who was having much too good a time seeing old friends.

"No problem," I replied.

The daughter gave a faint smile before returning to her father's casket.

"Not like the old days is it, Mavis," croaked June, "when we used to place our dead in the living room until the funeral?"

"It got to be too much if they died during the summer," mused Mavis.

Both ladies cackled.

"I remember sitting up all night with my grandmother before they put her in the ground," recalled June.

"Why did you do that?" I asked.

Both old crones looked at me as though I was a rather pretty but stupid pet.

"Robbers," said Mavis. "They'd steal in your house and take the jewelry right off the dead."

"Sometimes, they'd even take the bodies and sell them to medical facilities," chimed in June.

"This sounds very Dickensian to me," I challenged.

"Only uptown people could afford to let the funeral home keep the bodies until the burial, and even then, a family member would stay to keep an eye on the funeral home staff."

"In the deep South, the staff would cut the hair and fingernails off the deceased and sell it to the voodoo priests. Sometimes they even cut off fingers to use in dark magic," detailed June.

Mavis nodded in agreement.

"Whatever," I murmured.

June went on, "I hope it's my first husband who comes for me when my time comes. I miss him so."

I countered, "I thought the love of your life was Arthur . . ."

"Shush," hissed June. "The dead do come for you."

Mavis sniffed. "Oh, I see that Josiah is too educated to believe in the old ways, but I can tell you first hand that Terrence died after Mama came for him."

June grabbed Mavis' gnarled hands. "Really. Your mother came for him?"

I snorted with derision. I don't know why. Hadn't Brannon come for me after I had fallen off the cliff and was near death? Why was I being such a booger? Guess I'm ornery, that's all.

Both women looked at me with scorn.

"Tell me what happened, Mavis. I've got to know if there's an afterlife. I'll be going soon myself and it would be a comfort to know that a loved one would come for me."

"That's just it, June. Terry hated Mama. She always berated him while living. I think it was just an odd choice to send her."

I bit my tongue trying to be diplomatic for once. I wanted to know why Mavis didn't think her mother had come for her. "Why do you think your mama came for Terry?" I asked.

Mavis blew her nose in an overused hanky. "Something was bothering him. Something fierce, but he wouldn't tell me what it was. It started at your

Valentine party, June. He was happy when we got there
and then jumpy afterwards."

I suddenly became interested, as the purpose of the
Valentine party was to introduce Jean Louis to Bluegrass
society.

I didn't like Jean Louis. His lips said one thing, but
his eyes said something else. Jean Louis was always
asking questions, snooping.

Hey! Wait a minute. That sounds like me!

I didn't trust him and had been keeping an eye on him
until Matt had been shot, then gave up. I had other
priorities.

"What do you think was bothering him, Mavis?"
asked June, greatly concerned. "Did someone say
something to Terry that upset him? Had you been cattin'
around on him?"

Mavis gave a brief smile at the last suggestion. "What
a ridiculous idea at my age!" She shook her head. "Like I
said, he wouldn't tell me."

"Can you pinpoint exactly during the party when
Terry became upset," I asked. "It might be important."

Mavis put a finger to her lips in thought. "Well, I was
talking to Mrs. Dupuy about the robbery last Christmas
when Terry interrupted us, saying he wanted to go home.
He was very insistent."

"What had he been doing?"

Mavis spoke to June. "You know how he loved art.
He was going into each of the rooms that were open for
the party and looking at the artwork, saving the library for
the last to look at your portrait. Of course, the portrait

wasn't finished, but he wanted to see the sketching on the canvas."

"Was he coming from the library?" I inquired.

"He was coming from the direction of the library, but I first saw him near the staircase," recounted Mavis, closing her eyes to help her remember the scene. "But I can't tell you for sure if he had been in the library."

"And?" I prompted.

"It wasn't too long after that Mother started showing up at night. Oh, it gave us both a terrible fright. We weren't sure what she wanted. She would never say. Just stood in the corner of the bedroom looking . . . how shall I put it? This is terrible to say about one's own mother, but she looked creepy."

"To say the least," comforted June.

"It turned out she wanted Terry. He had a heart attack several weeks after the haunting." Mavis blew her nose again. "You'd think she'd come for me. I'm her blood."

"She might still, Mavis," I predicted.

Mavis jerked her head up. "Oh?" She didn't like that idea at all.

"What did Terry do between the party and your mother's appearance?" I asked.

"He was on the Internet constantly and then going to the library looking up old newspaper stories." Mavis blew her nose again.

"Do you know what about?" questioned June, handing Mavis a hanky from her purse.

Mavis was becoming somewhat untidy with all the nose blowing. She wiped her nose, looking at the both of us with wide, red-rimmed brown eyes that glistened with unspent tears. "Yes. He was investigating art thefts."

I started to ask about this when Mavis' son-in-law came to fetch her.

It was not the right time to question Mavis. The subject of art theft had certainly gotten my attention. That was a bone this dog would definitely dig up.

4

Here it was.

The conversation I dreaded.

I knew I was going to face a devil of a time, but it was already taking a nasty turn. There was just no talking sense to Franklin when it concerned Matt.

Matt was my best friend since my divorce from Brannon. We met at a party where I helped him win a bet about an old movie. Since then we had been as thick as thieves.

Franklin had been Matt's partner until Matt decided to marry Meriah Caldwell. You see how this is a complicated matter.

Matt didn't marry Meriah because a crazy woman committed a murder/suicide at their nuptials. That would put a pall over any ceremony. In the end, Meriah decided not to marry Matt but there was one small issue.

Meriah was pregnant.

I know this sounds like a soap opera, but life is messy like a soap opera.

Matt stayed. Meriah flew back to Los Angeles.

Then, while helping a friend recover her son's body, Matt and I were attacked by O'nan, that rogue cop I was telling you about. He shot Matt and then tried to drown me in the Cumberland River, but someone shot him with a sniper rifle. His body was recovered at the bottom of Cumberland Falls. He was dead, but the damage was done.

The doctors are not sure that Matt will ever recover. So I had made the decision to send Matt to Meriah because she had the money to take care of him . . . and now I was telling Franklin.

"And he's gone. Just like that."

I nodded. "He left last night on a chartered plane. I got word this morning that he arrived safely in Los Angeles and is okay. Everything went smoothly."

Franklin patted Baby, who had lodged his big head on Franklin's lap.

Baby whined and looked at Franklin with his big eyes,

only one of which could see, as O'nan had wounded it when he shot the dog as a puppy. It's one of the many reasons I had hated O'nan.

When Franklin cast an irritable glance at him, Baby wagged his massive tail, thumping heavily against the couch. Baby knew something was wrong with Franklin and was trying to comfort him the only way he knew.

"Who gave you the right to make a decision like this?"

"I told you last week about the possibility that this might have to happen. I called several times, but you never returned my calls, so I went ahead."

Franklin stared at me with complete disgust. "I mean, who gave you the legal right to make such a decision, to send a gravely ill man clear across the country? He could have died en route."

"Matt gave me Power of Attorney. I am his legal guardian if he is incapacitated, as he is mine. You know that, Franklin. When I fell off the cliff, he was making all the difficult decisions until Asa arrived."

"You never left us alone," Franklin accused. "You got Matt to live here. You slept with him. You were constantly interfering in our lives. We could have made a go of it, if you had stayed out of the picture."

"Franklin, listen to me. Matt wanted to live here. He didn't like city living. The truth is that Matt and I were close long before you came into the picture. I could say that you interfered with my relationship with Matt."

"You are such a liar. You seduced him."

"I feel very guilty that my relationship with Matt stepped over normal boundaries on your watch, but that it happened–no. It was a wonderful experience . . . one that I will cherish for the rest of my life."

I grabbed his hands and refused to let go. "Franklin, don't turn away. He needs constant care if he is going to recover. His insurance will not cover that. The nursing care is only for a few hours a day. Matt was going to be released from the hospital. He didn't have the medical backup he needed and I'm not strong enough to have cared for him."

"I could have helped."

"No, Franklin. You have a job. You have a life, friends. Matt would not have let you give up your daily routine to help him recover. He's too proud."

"I love him."

"I love him too, but did you ever think that our love is a burden? Did you ever think that Matt wants to be free of us?"

A tear escaped Franklin's eye.

"Meriah has more money than God. She can afford to pick up what the insurance won't cover. She has placed him in her guesthouse and he has around-the-clock nursing care. Plus, he has a reason to be there. She is going to give birth to his baby in a few weeks. Surely that will give Matt a reason to recover, a reason to live. That baby will give Matt strength."

"He won't ever come back. Meriah will get her claws into him."

"We're no good for Matt."

Franklin stood up. "You're no good for Matt. I've had nothing but misery since I've known you. Shootings and accidents that a normal person should not go through. You're a jinx, Josiah Reynolds; a bloody noose around our necks. And you've destroyed us. Came between me and the only person I will ever love. God, I hate you. I really hate you!" Franklin rushed out of the house, slamming the door.

Baby looked at me with a confused expression.

"Let him go, Baby. Let him go," I murmured. "He'll be back when he sees that I made the right decision."

But what worried me was that Franklin might be right. Maybe I was a jinx.

5

"I take it that it didn't go well," suggested June when I plumped down on the bed next to her.

I had a bottle of Pappy Van Winkle, the most expensive bourbon made, which I had swiped out of the downstairs liquor cabinet. I could never afford it and had spent some time drinking it in the den before taking the elevator to her ladyship's bedroom where June was currently ensconced.

I took a swig, shuddering slightly when the golden brown liquid hit my system. "He hates me. And I don't blame him, June. I would hate me, too."

"Franklin will get over it."

I shook my head. "I don't think so. This runs very deep with him. Franklin feels betrayed by both Matt and I. I mean me. No, it is I. Isn't it? His love for Matt is what Franklin says it is. I think Matt is the only man Franklin will ever love and I just sent his lover boy thousands of miles out of reach."

"Grammatically, it's me. You did what was best for Matt. He must realize that Matt wanted to go. Helped make the decision."

"Franklin doesn't want to see that. It's all my fault." I took another swig.

"Oh, well. 'Time heals all wounds.' "

" 'It is easier to forgive a friend . . .' "

"Ah, here we go," scoffed June.

"No, it goes like this . . . 'it is easier to forgive an enemy than forgive a friend.' William Blake."

" 'Et tu, Brute?' Shakespeare."

" 'You betray me with a kiss?' Jesus."

June reached for her bottle of bourbon and poured some into her tea. " 'We have to distrust each other. It's our only defense against betrayal.' Tennessee Williams."

" 'It is all right to rat . . . you just can't re-rat.' Winston Churchill."

"What does that mean?"

"I think he was referring to switching political parties."

"Hardly the type of betrayal we are talking about."

"You're so right," I chirped, grabbing the bottle back

from her Ladyship. "Okay. 'If I had to choose between betraying my country and betraying my friend, I hope I should have the guts to betray my country.' Edward M. Forster."

" 'Betrayal is the only truth that sticks.' Arthur Miller."

" 'Dealing with backstabbers, there was only one thing I learned. They're only powerful when you got your back turned.' "

"Who said that?"

"Eminem."

"M&M? Isn't that awfully clever for a piece of candy?"

"I think it's part of the Mars candy mission statement." And after taking yet another swig of Pappy's, I promptly passed out.

6

I awoke to find myself nicely tucked into June's massive bed. "Jumping Jehosaphat!" I moaned. "I feel like last year's rat poop."

Stumbling out of bed, I called for June, but no one answered. I smelled her perfume lingering in the room, so she had to have been here recently.

Was it already dark outside? I looked for a clock by the bed. It was after eight. Mercifully, I hadn't planned anything for that night, but there was a dog waiting that surely had to pee-pee.

After tinkling, washing my face, and using the last of June's mouthwash, I took the elevator downstairs.

The house was dark except for an occasional hallway light scattering the gloom here and there, and it was eerily quiet.

I called out, but no one answered.

In the kitchen I found a glass of water and a note tucked under a bottle of aspirin.

It was written in June's shaky handwriting,

Don't take too many, Dearie. Remember Addison DeWitt. I still love you, even if no one else does. June
PS. Leftovers in fridge. Better than what you have at home, I bet.

Hmmm. Looking in the fridge, I found several microwave containers with my name on them. Rather than take them home, I popped them in the microwave and nuked them. I also poured myself some iced tea.

The microwave beeped. Taking out one container, I popped in another. After taking some aspirin and downing a full glass of tea, I opened the first container. Eggplant Parmesan with garlic bread. Lovely and yummy. Ate that up quick.

Now for the second container. I slowly opened the seal.

Pot Roast!! Jackpot!!!

I groaned as I savored the first few bites. What's this? My head was no longer pounding. I actually felt like a human being again. Time to go home. I would share the leftover bounty with my friend, Baby.

Picking up the food container, I went into the hallway. "Bye!" I called. "And thanks."

No one answered.

"Anyone here?" I cried.

The silence was deafening.

That's when a little idea took shape in my head. Usually when those little ideas creep into my Wiener Schnitzel, Matt is standing in front of me saying no. But Matt was not here. Matt was in Los Angeles with a hot nurse giving him sponge baths while I was struggling in the Kentucky winter which wouldn't break for nuttin'.

Putting the food container on a hallway table, I crept down the main hallway and knocked on the library door. Hearing no response, I slowly peeked around the door and found the library empty.

Now, isn't this special!

Turning on the lights, I made straight for Jean Louis' painting collection, turning each one over and studying the painting. It was a vast collection and there didn't seem to be a theme. Each one was unique. They were paintings of different sizes, different eras, countries, and painting styles. I flipped each painting over, checking the canvas and stretchers in the back before inhaling their scent. Some of them were loose in their frames, making it easy to pop them out. Several of them had new canvas sewn onto the old canvas, which indicated to me that the original canvas had been cut too small for the current stretcher. That was not a good sign.

"Can I help you?"

Almost dropping the painting I was holding, I swung around to see Jean Louis standing behind me holding my food container.

"I didn't think anyone else was at home and it would be the perfect time for me to see your collection."

"Simply enjoying the paintings or studying for an insurance appraisal?"

"I *was* an art history professor."

"When one can't paint, she teaches," he muttered with contempt under his breath. Jean Louis handed my food container over as he took back the painting, placing it with the others. "I prefer to be present when others are viewing my treasures. Surely you can understand my apprehension."

"I'm sorry if I intruded. Have you been in the house all along? I called out several times."

"I have a key," he confided, holding up one of the house keys, "and the security code. I came to work on Lady Elsmere's portrait while she's out at a dinner party. I get more work done if I am left uninterrupted. Why are you in the house?"

I shrugged. "I got smashed and passed out."

"Charming."

"Well, thank you for the food. I'll be off now."

"You left the hot container on one of her Ladyship's antique tables. I'm afraid it has left a severe mark on the varnish."

"Great. Another triumph for the day." I waved goodbye with the container. "Thank you again. I'll let myself out. No need to bother locking up after me. I have my own key too."

I backed out of the library, never taking my eyes off Jean Louis. I didn't trust him, but I didn't know why. It was just a feeling.

Hurrying, I rushed to the kitchen and found the mayonnaise in the fridge. Snatching paper towels, I hurried into the hallway and rubbed some mayonnaise on the damaged table and then put a paper towel over it. "Oh, I hope this works or this is a cheap reproduction," I mumbled to myself.

I gave the table one last look before returning to the kitchen and putting everything back, but not before I lifted a bowl of fresh salad . . . and then some homemade ranch dressing . . . and then another of Bess' chocolate pies. The plate had only a few pie slices left. The meringue was starting to weep.

Satisfied that the fridge held no more treasures for me, I hastily wrote a note for Bess about the table and then left by the back door. In my defense, I didn't have anything to eat at home and was starving.

Bess would forgive me.

To be positive, I would stay away from the Big House for a couple of days. I surely had worn out my welcome for the time being.

7

The next day I was up early executing the list of errands that Eunice had scheduled for me. I was determined to return by early afternoon to help her write checks for the bills we owned. Hopefully, she would tell me that we had a tidy little profit for the month.

But as I headed into town, I thought I would look in on Mavis. I pulled into her driveway just behind her big-ass Cadillac. I wondered if she were going to sell it, as I doubted she could see over the dashboard. It was really Terry's car.

Mavis met me at the door. "Come in. Come in. Get out of this weather." She sniffed the air. "You breathe that, Josiah? Spring's right around the corner. The earth smells like it's turning."

I inhaled deeply. The air did smell different. "I just stopped by for a moment to see how you were doing."

"I'm doing fine. Still in shock I guess, but not defeated. I'll be with my Terrence when my time comes." Mavis gave me a knowing wink.

"I'm not going to sit down. Just staying for a few minutes. I'm on my way into town. Do you need anything?"

Mavis thought for a moment. "No. The pantry and freezer are full. I could never leave home and still have a different meal for a month." She gave a faint laugh.

"Mavis, have you thought of anything else about Terry's behavior at the party?" I asked abruptly.

Mavis looked at me in surprise. "Funny you should mention that. I was going through some of Terry's clothes and found a little notebook in one of his coat pockets." She reached down and pushed aside her crossword books until she found a little black notebook. "At first I though he had jotted down some names of horses he wanted to bet on." She handed it to me. "Now I'm not so sure. Can't think of what it refers to."

"Can I hold onto this for awhile?"

Mavis gave a puzzled look. "I guess, but I want it back, hear."

"I understand. One more thing. Has Mama visited you again?"

"Haven't seen her since Terry died, but I'll show you where she stood, if you'd like."

"Very much so." I followed Mavis into the bedroom.

Mavis pointed to a nondescript corner of the room. "She favored that spot."

I went over to the corner and moved the fake ficus tree out of the way. I felt the walls and stamped on the floor. Everything seemed as it should. Peeking between the venetian blinds, I peered out the window. Just a normal looking back yard, but with lots of places to hide. "Do you shut the blinds at night?"

"Nobody lives behind us. Just cattle behind the tree line."

"Does that mean no?"

"I guess so."

"No as in you don't close the blinds, or you leave them shut?"

"We always left the blinds open. Sometimes the window as well. We have a dog. He lets us know when somebody is around."

"Where is he now?"

"My daughter has him. Right before Terry died, our baby started feeling kind of puny, gasping for breath, vomiting. We took him right to the vet. The funny thing was that his nails took on a bluish color. I thought it best if he was checked out."

"Blue nails did you say?"

"Yep."

"Is he okay?"

"Yes, thank the Lord. He is staying with my daughter until things settle down. I don't feel up to taking care of a dog just yet. But I do want him back."

"I see you have a cat," I said, referring to the fat orange tabby lying on the bed.

He opened his golden eyes, giving us a baleful stare for interrupting his nap.

"Did the cat get sick like the dog?"

"No, just the dog, thank goodness."

"Mavis, what was the official cause of death for Terry?"

"Heart attack."

"Do you think seeing your mother brought it on?"

Mavis shook her head. "No, he was acting funny before she arrived. I just think his time was up and she came for him."

"How many times did you actually see her?"

"Three nights. In a row. We'd wake up and see her for a few minutes and then she'd fade away."

"Did she say anything?"

"No."

"Did you say anything to her?"

"I asked why she was in our bedroom the first night. On the second night I asked where she had hid her fudge recipe."

"What'd she say?"

"Nothing. Made me mad. I've been looking for that recipe since she passed away."

"Did she make eye contact?"

"No. The way she was turned in the corner made it look like she was staring at this painting."

I studied the painting on the wall. "It's *Landscape with Obelisk* by Govaert Flinck, isn't it?" I inquired.

"Of course, this is a reproduction. You understand the significance of it, don't you?"

"It's famous, but I don't remember why."

"The original was stolen from the Isabella Stewart Gardner Museum in Boston. It's one of the most famous art thefts in the world."

I snapped my fingers. "That's right. It's never been recovered. If I remember correctly, twelve other works were stolen as well. Is there a specific reason that you have a copy of it?"

"Then you don't know?"

"Know what?"

"We used to live in Boston and Terry was a guard at the Gardner Museum. Terry was there the night the museum was robbed."

8

You could have bowled me over with a feather.
Eunice's errands were going to have to wait.

"That's astounding. Might I have something to drink,
please? If you've got time, I'd like to hear all about it," I
babbled.

"I thought you were in a hurry."

"I'll tell Eunice I had car trouble or something to that
effect. You must tell me about Terry. I had no idea."

"He didn't like to talk about it," said Mavis, going into
the kitchen. "I have Coke or water. I can make coffee if
you like."

"Coke would be fine." I had to wait patiently as
Mavis pulled one of her good glasses from the cupboard,

put ice in it and then opened the Coke, slowly pouring into the glass, taking her time to let the fizzle die down before pouring more Coke. Satisfied, she handed the glass to me and we went to sit in the living room.

I politely took a sip while waiting for Mavis to spill the beans.

She took a long breath and began a story that had seldom slipped through her lips. "We lived in Boston."

I nodded in concurrence.

"Terry was a guard at the Isabella Stewart Gardner Museum. He liked working there. The staff was nice and Terry had a fondness for the art. One of his favorite paintings was the *Landscape with Obelisk*.

"One day, his supervisor asked him if he would work the night shift as one of the night guards had called in sick. Terry said he would, as we needed the extra money. That was March 18, 1990."

"What happened?" I asked breathlessly.

"He came home at his usual time, took a two-hour nap and then went back for the night shift. Everything was normal until two Boston cops showed up saying they were responding to a call. Terry was making his rounds so the guard at the front desk thought that maybe Terry had made the call and let the cops through the security door.

"But once the policemen got inside, all hell broke loose. They pulled out their guns and ordered the front door guard away from the desk where the panic button was, saying they had a warrant for his arrest. They handcuffed him and then made him summon Terry.

"Once Terry came up front, they overpowered him and handcuffed him too. Then the thieves took them both down to the basement where they duct-taped their hands and feet to pipes.

"They weren't found until the next morning. It was a miracle that they weren't killed, but Terry felt terribly guilty about the robbery. Of course, the police thought Terry and the other guard helped to execute the theft and gave Terry an awful time about it.

"We had to hire a lawyer. Finally the FBI concluded that he and the other guard had nothing to do with it, but we had already spent much of our savings on legal fees. Terry was so disgusted that we left Boston for good and decided to move where my people still lived. We came back to my mother's place until we could get back on our feet."

"How many paintings were stolen?"

"It was a collector's theft. Only specific items were taken from two floors. Five drawings by Degas, a finial for a pole support for a Napoleonic flag, a Chinese vase, a self-portrait of Rembrandt, and several other paintings."

"I can see why it is thought that a collector commissioned the robbery. The articles are so specific. Wood to porcelain, etchings to paintings. There doesn't seem to be a theme."

"And more expensive paintings were left behind."

"Some of the stolen items were not as well known," I said.

"Yes, Govaert Flinck is not an artist that most people would have known, unlike a Rembrandt or Degas. A regular person would recognize those names even if they had never had an art class in their lives, but only a real art hound would be familiar with a Flinck, but there was also a Manet and a Vermeer stolen as well. Both oils on canvas."

"That's quite a story," I uttered.

"Terry wanted it kept quiet, so we never spoke of it. He didn't want people thinking he had something to do with the robbery, even though he had been cleared. But you know how people talk."

"Thank you for telling me. I will be discreet," I promised.

"I would appreciate that. I don't want Terry's name tarnished. It's just awful that he had to die without the robbery being solved."

"I'll go through his book and I'll let you know if I discover anything."

"Don't forget I want that notebook back, Josiah."

"I won't and thank you kindly for the Coke. I best be on my way. Miss Eunice is gonna skin me alive."

Mavis gave me a wan smile and muttered while opening the door, "I hope winter breaks soon. I can't wait to see the redbuds bloom." She looked wistfully at the cloudy sky, waved and then shut the front door.

9

Winter had finally broken. It was going to be in the mid-sixties for the next several days. Time to work with my bees.

I got Tyrone, one of Charles' grandsons, to help me. We suited up and finally got the smoker to work. Getting that smoker to smoke was the hardest thing about beekeeping for me. The smoke calmed the bees enough to let us work in relative peace.

I smoked the front entrance to the hive and then Tyrone lifted the outer cover so I could smoke the top of the hive. We gave the bees a minute and then Tyrone lifted the outer cover off the hive, putting it aside.

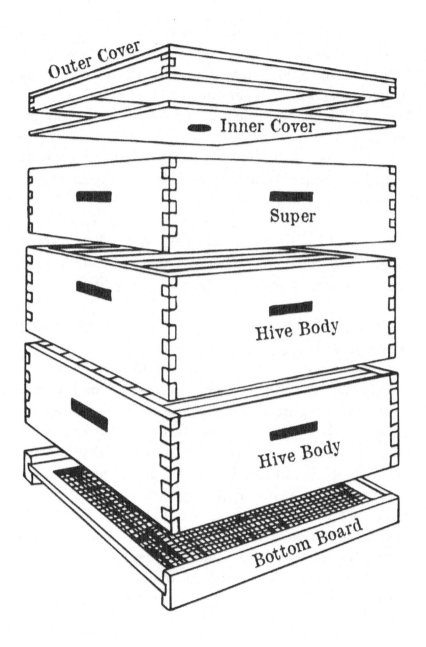

I smoked the hole of the inner cover and then Tyrone pried it off with a hive tool and put it on the ground. Again, I smoked down into the frames of the hive so that the bees would flee deeper into the hive. Handing Tyrone the smoker, I pried out a frame from the top hive body.

"The Queen's already laying," remarked Tyrone as we studied the capped brood pattern. It was large and oval. Perfect.

I put it back and pulled out another one. This one had a good brood pattern too, along with pollen in the upper cells. The maple trees must already be blooming. They were among the first trees to come to life in Kentucky.

"There's the Queen!" cried Tyrone excitedly, pointing to one of the bees.

I looked closely at her. It was rare to see a Queen. Usually they hid. She was gliding along looking for an empty cell to lay an egg in, oblivious to the fact that she was out in the open away from the dark safety of her hive. House bees corralled her as if to protect her from the sunlight. She looked healthy. A good Queen could lay 2000 eggs a day during the high season. I put the frame back carefully. The last thing I wanted to do was disturb the Queen.

"Let's switch the hive bodies. You pull the top hive body off while I pull off the bottom hive body," I instructed.

The bees had glued the two boxes together with propolis, which is glue they make from tree sap and beeswax.

I worked the boxes free of the propolis with my hive tool. "I think I got them free. On the count of three. One two three."

Tyrone pulled the heavy top hive body off and placed it on an outer cover. That way we wouldn't lose the Queen in the grass.

I smoked the bottom hive body and pulled out some frames. As expected, the cells were empty of eggs or capped brood. All the bees had moved into the top hive body. I pulled off the empty hive body.

Tyrone placed the top hive body full of bees on the bottom board.

I then poured powdered sugar onto the frames and all the bees that came up to investigate. Using powdered sugar was controversial, but I had found it effective to use against mites. While combing the powder from their fur, parasitic mites would fall to the bottom and out of the hive through the bottom screen.

After I powdered the bees, Tyrone lifted the empty hive body on top of the loaded hive box. Got that? We just switched hive boxes. Put the bee heavy top body on the bottom and the empty hive body on top.

I then put pollen patties on the top frames and shut the hive by replacing the inner and outer covers.

More beekeepers lose bees from starvation in the spring than from any other cause, which is why I put pollen patties in the hive for the bees to eat.

Grabbing some duct tape out of my kit, I wrapped it around the seams of the two hive bodies so predators couldn't get to the food we had just placed inside.

The bees would now have the calories they needed to hunt for nectar and fresh pollen while raising new baby bees.

I needed at least one hundred thousand bees in each hive to get a good harvest.

Bees usually make around four hundred to five hundred pounds of honey per year, but they eat most of it. And I left one hundred pounds of honey in the hives to get them through winter. That gave me about fifty pounds of honey to harvest.

Satisfied that the hive was healthy and the Queen was active, I went on to the next hive. We repeated the same steps with each hive until I came to one that smelled like moldy yeast.

"Do you think it's American Foulbrood?" asked Tyrone.

Foulbrood was the hoof-and-mouth disease of the bee world. Usually the hive had to be destroyed before it infected the other hives.

I took a toothpick and picked at one of the drone cells. "No, it's not ropy. The hive sure smells funny though." I sniffed again. "I think some of the honey is last year's aster honey. Let's just treat them like normal. Perhaps the extra energy from the pollen patties will help them clean out their hive and get them on a normal path. We'll check again in a few days and see if the smelly honey is gone. If not, then we'll go from there."

"How do you like being free?" asked Tyrone, changing the topic. "We're out here working the bees. You haven't jumped once. Not looking over your shoulder. You don't have to worry about O'nan anymore."

I smiled bitterly. "At times I feel nothing but sorrow over the past events and other times I feel like doing a jig 'cause that mother is dead. You know, the usual conflicting emotions anyone would have . . . regret, relief, and rhapsody." I shrugged my shoulders. "How do you feel? It affected you too."

"I just would have shot him. Bang. Just like that. You're dead."

"Well, that's what finally happened. Someone got fed up with O'nan's threats and shot him."

"Was it you? Come on. You can tell me. You're part of my posse. I won't tell."

"Tyrone, you're the max," I replied, looking at his innocent face. "You know I didn't do it."

Tyrone sidled up to me. "Was it Asa? Did you have Asa ice him for you?"

"She was out of the country when it happened. She has witnesses."

Looking at Tyrone's crestfallen demeanor, I chuckled, "I always thought you were the one who did the evil deed."

The young man returned a beaming smile. "I thought about it. Dreamed about it. Me and my posse."

"That being your brother and cousins?"

"We talked about it, but Grandpa said no. He threatened to disinherit us so we stopped . . . well, at least where he could hear."

"And he was so right," I laughed, wishing I was so enthusiastic about something again. Why is youth wasted on the young?

"Who do you suspect?"

"I haven't the faintest, but you know what? I just don't give a damn. I'm glad that someone finally had the guts to put that rabid dog down. Too many have suffered due to him."

"Think that you're ever gonna find out?" asked Tyrone, putting bee equipment back into my old golf cart.

I shook my head. "I hope not, dear boy. I hope not."

"My Grandma says secrets never stay hidden in Kentucky . . . that either the water or the dirt just spits secrets back up to God."

I shivered at his words.

"You cold?"

"No. It felt like someone just walked over my grave."

We both looked at the deep woods surrounding the bee yard. It was quiet except for the leaves gently rustling in the afternoon breeze.

Too quiet.

No birds calling. No cows bellowing in the distance. No tractors working the land. No airplanes going overhead. Not even the bees could be heard buzzing.

Suddenly spooked, we both jumped into the golf cart and raced out of the field.

To my surprise, I found myself looking fearfully over my shoulder.

Oh, snap!

10

I was spooked.

Before checking the security systems, I let in Baby's pets . . . the Kitty Kaboodle Gang as I call the clowder of barn cats. I was going to call them Pussies Galore after the character in the James Bond *Goldfinger* movie until Franklin kept asking if he could kiss my pussies.

Ah, Franklin. What a rake.

Going into the kitchen, I realized that I was hungry. I went into the walk-in freezer and pulled out a wrapped Bybee dish.

I peeked under the wrapper. Yum. Homemade meatloaf with mashed potatoes and creamed corn. I nuked it with hearty glee.

The buzzer of the microwave chirped and I took the steaming dish with a glass of water into my office. As I walked along the wide corridor, shadows seemed to dance across the slate and concrete floor.

I heard Baby pad down the hallway after smelling the meatloaf. I had left him in the kitchen struggling to keep the cats out of his food bowl. It seemed that his buddies had taken a liking to dog food . . . Baby's food, and with his inability to deny his friends anything, Baby always came up short. Now he was on the prowl looking for other sustenance.

Rather than listen to Baby whine, I gave him a piece of meatloaf. "Careful," I cautioned. "It's still hot."

Baby gulped the meatloaf down only to lick my ketchup-covered fingers. I wiped my hand on my pants.

Except for Baby's gulping and slurping, the Butterfly was quiet. Too quiet. It was unnerving.

I realized that I was alone. Really alone in the world.

After Brannon had left, Matt came into my life and filled the void of a male companion. Then I met Franklin, who was all sparkle and fun. Then I fell in love with Jake.

Now they were gone.

Asa was in London. Besides June and Eunice or an occasional social invitation, I didn't see anyone. There was no one to confide in or talk over the highs and lows of the day's experiences.

I was lonely. I was afraid of growing old alone. I was fearful that my luck would run out.

Suddenly I wasn't hungry anymore. Bending over, I placed the Bybee dish on the floor.

Baby dived in happily.

I watched him eat with relish and joy.

The Kitty Kaboodle Gang, in their desire for mischief, bounced into the office and began climbing everything they could get their claws into, plus scattering paper off my desk and reclining on my keyboard.

Finished with dinner, Baby wiped his mashed potato crusty face on my pants and then stuck his snout in my crotch so I could scratch his ears.

I suddenly felt ashamed. If Baby, after three bullet wounds, could love and live his life with relish, who was I to sit on my pity-pot.

Pity-pot. That reminded me of another pity-pot. My grandmother who used to say, "Either you-know-what or get off the pot."

"You're a good friend, Baby," I cooed as I scratched his ears. "Yes, you are. Yes, you are."

Baby responded by thumping his tail loudly against the desk.

"You're a good example of how to live one's life."

When Baby looked up at me, I swear he was smiling.

"You live in the moment. You suffer no regrets. You forget about the past. I wish I could be more like you. If you stumble, you put the other paw in front and keep on trotting. You're my inspiration."

Picking up a cat from my keyboard, I placed it on Baby's back. "Now, go play with your friends. Mommy's got to work."

Baby went to lie by the door, as Mastiffs were prone to do. They had been trained to guard the entrance to the castle keep for so many centuries, it was now in their blood.

I opened a browser and keyed in "art thefts."

Art thieves seem to be of an incompetent nature, as they do such a bad job of disposing of the stolen works. Unless the paintings or rare objects are for a private collector, the loot is usually too hot to sell. Invariably, paintings worth millions are stored in someone's attic or placed in a yard sale. Or they are recycled to other museums. OOOPS!

The J. B. Speed Museum in Louisville–that is pronounced "Louavul"–paid $38,000 to the Newhouse Galleries in New York in 1973 for a triptych depicting the Virgin Mary. It had been painted by Jacopo del Casentino who died in 1358.

Unknown to them, the triptych had been stolen and was ultimately tracked down by an Italian scholar in 2011. It seemed word had gotten back to the owners of the triptych that their stolen property was being ogled by Kentucky swells on a daily basis. Gee–how embarrassing for the Speed Museum.

The seventies seemed like the banner decade for stealing artwork. In 1973, two Rembrandt paintings, valued at two million dollars at the time, were lifted from the Taft Museum in Cincinnati, Ohio, a Midwestern town with Germanic heritage only two hours on I-75 north of the little Southern town of Lexington.

A ransom of $200,000 was asked. Apparently, the thieves didn't realize what they had, but of course, $200,000 in 1973 was a lot of money for a poor robber.

Make that poor and stupid. Two days later, one of the Rembrandts was found in a barn and the second painting was discovered in a vacant house within the week. Very poor planning if you ask me.

However, one of the most spectacular heists happened in my own little Bluegrass backyard. In 1994, a professional group of thieves stole one hundred and three bibelots and artwork worth $1.6 million dollars at the time.

Well, that's not much, you say.

It was not what they stole, but from whom they stole.

A gang known as the Waterford Rats crept into the Headley-Whitney Museum on July 17, thinking that this score would gain them entrance into the Mafia. What dumb asses!

Who are the Headleys and the Whitneys, you may ask.

The Headley-Whitney Museum was started by George Headley on his farm, La Belle. In the forties, Headley opened his own jewelry boutique at the Hotel Bel-Air in Los Angeles, catering to the Hollywood elite like Judy Garland, Fannie Brice, Joan Crawford, and Gary Cooper. Pining for home, Headley returned to La Belle and continued designing jewelry and bibelots. (Bibelots are decorative curios made of precious jewels and metals, and are to be displayed rather than worn.)

One spectacular bibelot was a platinum parachutist attached to a parachute of diamonds. How precious!

In 1960, he married Barbara Whitney, daughter of sculptor Gertrude Vanderbilt Whitney, who founded the Whitney Museum of Art in New York City.

Barbara Whitney's brother was Cornelius Vanderbilt Whitney III, an original investor in Pan Am Airlines and a financial backer for *Gone With The Wind*. He was very instrumental in getting the censors to allow Clark Gable to utter the famous line, *"Frankly, my dear, I don't give a damn."* Damn was considered an unforgivable curse word in 1939.

Just like his brother-in-law, George, Cornelius had his own little horse farm in Lexington–just around one thousand acres of the best dirt in the country and was home to more than four hundred stakes winners.

So you see that these people were movers and shakers–Bluegrass aristocracy who were lovers of art and beauty. One does not steal from the powerful and wealthy without paying a price.

Still, no number of private detectives or law enforcement agents could break the case until a James P. Quinn was arrested on an unrelated burglary charge and in return for a plea deal, confessed to the theft. He was part of the Waterford Rats, who had stolen over ten million dollars worth of goods in Kentucky, Ohio, and Florida.

I guess they worked Florida in the winter.

What happened to George Headley's precious collection?

James Quinn said they couldn't fence the collection, so they broke the bibelots apart and what they couldn't break, they melted down and then sold for a fraction of what the artwork was worth. I never said they were smart thieves.

Hmmm. This was very fascinating and interesting, but nothing seemed to fit the description of Jean Louis' collection. The new canvas stitched onto the old canvas was a dead giveaway that something was not right with his collection.

I checked the FBI list of stolen art objects.

Oh dear. That was not going to work. The number of missing or stolen artworks was overwhelming. I was going to need specific information if I saw this through, and I was not even sure if his paintings were stolen. Jean Louis could be totally honest and legit.

It was just that my nose was twitching.

And then there was the visitation from his mother-in-law just before Terry's untimely death.

If you asked if I believed in ghosts, I would tell you no.

If you asked if I had ever seen a ghost, I would say yes.

Why the contradiction?

I don't really understand how a ghost could exist. When you're dead, you're dead.

But I can tell you that I saw Brannon, my late husband, three times after my fall off the cliff. He spoke to me and I could even smell his aftershave.

Terry saw his mother-in-law for three nights. In fact, I believe that his mother-in-law came from the Great Beyond to warn him.

But I don't believe in ghosts.

Most people in Kentucky don't believe in ghosts, but almost everyone has seen one.

11

I had just finished reading Edgar Allan Poe's *The Purloined Letter* when Baby rose from napping at my feet only to whine while pacing by the back windows.

"What is it, boy?" I asked, going over to the windows.

The treetops were swaying and the air had an odd yellowish glow about it. Uh oh! Not a good sign in Kentucky. A yellowish sky with green tints means tornadoes. Better turn on the radio.

Before I could, there was strong protesting in the form of caterwauling. I opened the patio door and in rushed Mama and the Kitty Kaboodle Gang, which then hurried to Baby for comfort. After Baby nuzzled them in greeting, they turned to me as if to say, "Now what?"

I went into the kitchen pantry where I kept pet carriers for emergencies. I put the protesting felines into the carriers and put a sturdy leash on Baby, wondering how I was going to manage him. He could be difficult when frightened and he was strong as a bull. Baby was just too much dog for me after my accident. I didn't have the strength to control him, but what could I do? I loved him.

The doorbell rang.

Great! Who could that be?

Amidst the cat meowing and hissing plus the dog barking and straining against the leash, in other words, general commotion, I managed to look at the security monitors.

Thank goodness.

I opened the door. "I thought you hated me."

"I do, but I adore Baby. I guess it finally dawned on you that a tornado is coming this way, Dorothy Gale."

"Auntie Em you're not, but I'm glad you didn't call me the Wicked Witch of the West."

"You should have heard me yesterday only I started the word witch with a 'b'. What's the game plan?"

"I usually go to the Big House."

"Why not stay here?"

"Because I don't have a basement filled with gourmet food, champagne, sleeping accommodations, and cable TV."

"See your point." Franklin looked behind him at the trees waving wildly around the house. "The wind is really picking up. Shall we go?"

"You take Baby and the cats and go on to the Big House. Just go in the back door. The stairway to the basement is in the butler's pantry."

"What are you going to do?" asked Franklin, looking anxiously at the sky.

Thunder sounded in the distance.

Baby began pulling at his leash and I was having difficulty holding onto him.

"I've got to open up the pastures. Then I'll help with June's horses. Don't worry. I'll be safe, but you can really help if you take Baby now."

Franklin looked dubious.

I handed him Baby's leash and the cat carriers. Thunder sounded again which caused Baby to panic. It took both Franklin and me to get him into the Smart Car. Franklin threw the cats in the back and, giving me one last look, took off to the Big House.

I got into the golf cart and sped toward the barns and pastures.

My farm is entirely closed in by fences with connecting gates. During tornadoes, I open each of the gates so the animals can run away from storms. Many take refuge in the woods where they feel safe.

My thought is that leaving an animal locked in a barn during a tornado is a possible death sentence.

I checked each barn and made sure no animal was trapped inside. After securing all the barn doors to be sure they stood open, I drove over to June's stables.

Unlike me, June had money enough to construct a barn built into a hillside with a large dirt ramp connecting to underground stalls. I caught up with Bess directing farmhands.

"Where's Mike?" I asked, referring to the farm manager.

"He's trapped at Keeneland. Can't get here. It's just me."

"Where do you need help?" I yelled at the top of my lungs. It was hard to see Bess as the wind was stirring up dust devils, which were dancing around the barn compound.

"The mares with the spring foals are the last," she hollered back, pointing at a nearby barn.

I nodded and directed my cart to the foaling barn, dodging panicking horses and farmhands. Many of the horses had blankets over their eyes.

Unlike me, Mike didn't like the horses outside during severe storms, so he brought them into the barns with the most valuable going into the special underground stalls. Of course, June's newer barns were extremely sturdy and constructed for tornadoes.

I didn't like June's policy, but it wasn't my call. She and Mike were doing what they thought was right for the safety of their horses.

Inside the barn were anxious farmhands trying to calm the mares enough to move them. I grabbed the halter of one of the mares and led her out of the stall, knowing that her foal would follow. Thank goodness she was a trusting animal. I got the mare and her baby into the underground barn and a secure stall without incident.

It was very important that the horses not be cut or scratched during their move. I quickly checked the mare, especially her legs, before reporting to Bess.

By that time, Bess had finished counting the horses. All were accounted for and secured. Now all that was needed was luck that the tornado skirted the property.

Most of the farm workers were staying in the underground barn where there was ample food and water for both man and horse. The men and women were already getting out cards to play poker. The spooky weather didn't faze them, as it occurred every spring. They were used to it.

Bess and I got into the golf cart and did one last sweep around the farm before heading back to the Big House.

As we crested a ridge, we saw a tornado in the distance heading toward us.

"Let's get out of here!!" cried Bess.

I made a beeline to the Big House and the cart had barely stopped moving before we jumped out, hurrying inside and downstairs.

You would barely know that there was a problem with the weather, given the calm in the shelter.

June and Franklin sat in a corner, both of them trying on June's massive jewelry collection, which she had brought down with her. Liam was making sandwiches in the basement kitchen while Charles' grandsons listened to the emergency radio. A TV blared in the corner.

Baby ran up to me and gave little barking sounds, apparently complaining that his cat friends had been placed in a storage room.

"Nice to see you too, Baby," I commented.

Tyrone spoke up, "If Baby's concerned about those cats, he shouldn't be. They have litter, cat food, and water. Plus there are toys with catnip."

"No problem. I know several of you have cat allergies. They'll be fine."

"Thanks for not causing a fuss," replied Tyrone, "like some people." He rolled his eyes at Jean Louis who was mumbling about the coffee not being hot.

Tornadoes can be very frightening for those who have never been threatened by one. Being a sucker for those in distress, I went over to Jean Louis and asked, "Do you want your coffee heated?"

"This savage country. Since I've been here my allergies have been intolerable, no decent brewed coffee or croissants and now this. My collection. What will become of my collection?"

"I see you brought the paintings with you. They will be safe as you will be. A tornado could rip this house apart, but we will be safe down here."

"Rip the house apart? Mon Dieu!"

Tyrone spoke up, "We get earthquakes, too. In fact, the largest earthquake ever in the U.S. was the New Madrid Earthquake of 1811-12. It was so strong the

Mississippi flowed backwards and church bells rang in Boston."

"Is that supposed to make me feel better?" snarled Jean Louis.

"Hush up, boy," snapped Bess. "No one needs to hear how smart you are."

Tyrone shrugged and returned to listening to the radio.

"I'd rather face a tornado than an earthquake. A tornado is random. Not everyone is affected, but an earthquake is different. Why, the earth could drop right out from underneath you," commented Franklin.

"Franklin, I'd take you a little more seriously if you weren't wearing a tiara and pendant earrings," I drawled.

"I'm not talking to you. I still hate you," hissed Franklin, putting on an emerald necklace.

"You don't hate me nor are you mad at me. You're furious with Matt and taking it out on me."

Franklin pulled off the earrings. "We were so good together. What happened?"

"He's got guilty feet," interrupted June as she rummaged through her jewelry box. "He was too good-looking and couldn't resist all the temptation coming his way. He thought Meriah might tether him to the ground."

"What the hell does that mean?" asked Franklin, yanking a sapphire bracelet off June's arm and putting it on his.

"It means that Matt didn't think he was good enough for you."

"Huh?"

June looked exasperated. "Really, for a smart person, you can be dense, Franklin. It is very simple.

"You are a good person. Matt isn't. Oh, he is suave, charming, hardworking, and beautiful, but he's not good. Matt is a user. He uses his charm and beauty and sex appeal to get what he wants from people. The only people he hasn't used are you and Josiah.

"He thought that with Meriah, who has everything that he wants . . . great wealth, material possessions, connections . . . he would stop wanting. Would stop using people as he would have all that he had previously aspired to obtain."

Franklin looked stunned. "I don't know what to say to that? I think of Matt as a good person."

"Which is why Matt left you. He knows what he is and is trying to change. Leave him alone, Franklin. Let him make the journey to redemption as he wishes."

I patted June's arm. "I sometimes forget what a smart old broad you are."

"Age does have its privileges like wisdom and power. You know, Josiah, that with great power comes great responsibility."

"Voltaire?"

"Uncle Ben in *Spiderman*," grinned June.

I opened my mouth to retort, but didn't get a chance, as that was when the tornado hit.

12

"What is that?" screeched Jean Louis, looking up at the ceiling.

Bess motioned for all of us to quiet down as she strained to listen.

The thunderous sound of a train roared down upon the Big House.

"Everyone in the corner, now!" ordered Bess as she herded us into the deep recesses of the basement.

I was pulling Baby by his collar until he bucked and wrestled of out it.

Franklin rescued us both by grabbing Baby's front paws and dragging him into the corner. Then Franklin threw himself on top of Baby.

I flung myself over both Franklin and Baby as the deafening tumult rushed over us.

The house shook as the lights went out, plunging us into darkness.

I was screaming along with Jean Louis.

13

Jean Louis kept screaming like a stuck pig until June reached over and boxed his ears. He then resorted to whimpering.

Remind me never to count on that man in an emergency.

Several seconds later it was quiet. I don't think even a minute had passed. It was very serene. It was as if the earth had stopped moving.

We all straightened from our crouched positions and stood listening to the silence until the emergency generator kicked on. The basement flooded with light again.

Bess immediately got on her walkie-talkie and called the farmhands in the underground barn. To our relief they answered and said they and the horses were all right.

"Is it over?" asked Jean Louis.

"For now," replied Bess.

"Bien," cried Jean Louis as he rushed up the stairs.

"You can't go out there, man!" yelled Tyrone, chasing Jean Louis. "There's a entire cell of storms in the area. More than one tornado. You can't go up top until they pass through."

"Go get that fool and bring him back," ordered Bess to the rest of her sons and nephews. "Tie him up if you have to."

I pulled June to her feet and straightened the lopsided tiara on her head. "Let me help you into a chair, Lady Elsmere," I offered.

"You have got to train that dog," accused Franklin, taking off jewelry. "He's too strong."

"I have tried, Franklin. He's been kicked out the best obedience training schools in the area. Baby is just obstinate. Is this really the time to go off about Baby?"

"Just look at me. There's drool everywhere. I'm a wet mess."

Baby licked Franklin's hand and then belched very loudly in his face.

"God, I love Kentucky," chirped June. "Where else do you get an evening's entertainment like this?"

Franklin gave me a strange look. "I don't think loss of property and life is entertainment, June," he admonished.

"It's the roll of the dice, boy. The roll of the dice," she replied.

He shrugged and went to check on the cats. Baby followed him. Of course, when he opened the door, all of the cats scampered out, much to Baby's delight.

"Who let those cats loose?" demanded Bess.

Franklin pointed at me.

14

"If it's not one thing, it's another. Put those cats up, Josiah, and put that dog with them," ordered Bess.

I gave Franklin a dirty look before scooping up a cat here and there.

I could tell that Bess was frustrated. She had a lot of responsibility on her shoulders and she did not want to let her father, Charles, down. After all, they would inherit the Big House and the farm once June passed away. That is, if June died of natural causes. Any hanky-panky with the cause of June's demise and the entire fortune went to charity.

I had to get my animals under control. It was only good manners on my part. I gave up on Baby having any manners of his own accord. I would have to resort to bribery.

This time Baby happily followed his feline friends into the storage room after I rattled a dish filled with dog food that I had stashed in one of the cat carriers.

Happily, Baby inhaled his food. I knew with a full belly, he would soon settle down. I petted Baby until his eyes drooped with sleep. The cats were already claiming their sleeping spots near or on him.

I quietly left and softly shut the storage room door.

While I had been putting Baby to bed, others had followed suit. People, who were either sleeping from exhaustion or nervously reading or watching the TV for further news, occupied the couches, cots, and air mattresses.

I sidled up to Bess, who was watching the latest weather report. "What happened to Jean Louis? He's out like a light," I said to Bess while studying Jean Louis snoring on one of the couches.

Bess gave me a wily grin. "I put two Benadryls in his coffee. Works every time."

"At least he'll wake up rested."

"And it won't be for a while."

Suddenly I got a crazy idea. "Bess, I'm going upstairs to get an aspirin. I've got a hell of a headache."

"Sorry that we don't have any down here. Take this flashlight just in case the lights go out again. There is a bottle of aspirin in the servants' bathroom by the kitchen. Now make sure you come right back. I don't want to be worrying about you."

"I'll be fine." I took the flashlight and headed upstairs. But I had no intention of coming right back.

15

It has always been my theory that when opportunity knocks, open the door, which is what I did. I opened the back door and stepped out into the storm.

The rain had stopped, but the wind whistled through the trees. All lights were out except for the solar barn lights and those in the Big House.

I knew if I were going to do this, I would have to hurry. Not because Bess might come looking for me, but that another tornado might bounce onto the farm any moment.

Stepping up my pace, I skirted to the pool near the guest bungalow. The door was locked. Using the flashlight, I broke the glass in the door. No one would be suspicious, as they would think the storm caused the damage.

I unlocked the door and let myself in. Looking at my watch, I was going to give myself ten minutes before I went back.

First thing I did was go through Jean Louis' closet, searching his luggage and the pockets of his clothes. Nothing. Next, I went through his drawers. Nothing again. Surely there had to be something.

Then I saw it in the corner. His portfolio. Grabbing it, I laid it open on a table and took out all the drawings. I had learned a thing or two from Asa about how to search for contraband. Feeling around the edges of the portfolio I discovered a slight bump in the lining.

Worrying with it, I discovered that part of the lining was affixed to the frame of the portfolio with velcro. I pulled the velcro apart and felt inside. My fingers made contact with slick paper. Gingerly, I pulled it through the opening.

It was an old black and white photograph of a bride and her groom standing before an altar. The forties-era bride was beaming at her new husband, who was wearing a German Schutzstaffel uniform.

The dreaded German SS!

So much for Jean Louis' parents fighting in the French Resistance.

Of course they were his parents. He and the man in the picture shared the same beady eyes.

I flipped the picture over. Scribbled in German on the back was 22. Juni, 1941. (June 22, 1941.) Behind the beaming couple were hundreds of paintings stacked against the walls of the altar.

Carefully, I reinserted the photograph and closed the velcro. After placing Jean Louis' sketches in the order that I had found them, I put the portfolio back.

I realized now that I had a piece of the puzzle. And the photograph had made it possible.

I think the couple was showing off the soldier's work, which were the stacked paintings. My educated guess was this SS solider was a member or working with the Kunstschutz.

And what is the purpose of the Kunstschutz?
It was to confiscate art throughout Europe. In other words–steal it by hook or by crook.

How do I know this? I was an art history professor–remember?

16

Oscar Wilde once said, "Every saint has a past and every sinner has a future." Since Oscar Wilde was both a saint and sinner, I guess he should know.

Myself–I am a great believer in sin and redemption. I think it is a Southern thing. I am not above tweaking the rules here and there because I know *though my sins be as scarlet, they shall be white as snow,* Isaiah 1:18.

Every woman knows that if she played by the rules all the time, she'd never get anywhere, so I was ready to dip into my pocket of tricks to get Goetz to do what I wanted. After all, somewhere down the road, I would be forgiven for being a conniving she-devil . . . if I repented. The hard part for me was being truly sorry for my sins, as I firmly believed I had been sinned against more often than not.

"What do you want?" growled Detective Goetz.

Standing in the doorway of his office, I cooed, "Now, don't be that way. You know you're glad to see me. I don't know why you act like you hate me when we both know you don't. I just wanted to check up on you after the tornado." I strode into the office and plopped down in the chair opposite his desk. "Say you're sorry for being so rude."

Goetz rubbed his hound dog face. "You're right. I was rude."

I smiled my brightest smile.

"Now, what do you want?"

My smile dimmed. "Do I have to want anything? Can't I just stop by and see an old friend? A friend whom I have helped solve his cases. Remember how I broke my leg?"

"It was a stress fracture. Not broken at all."

"And almost got my head caved in with a shovel," I continued.

"I would like to have a dollar for every time I have gotten your butt out of trouble."

"I wish I had a dime for every time I got *your* butt out of trouble."

"Did you bring me something to eat?"

"Is this what the grouchiness is all about? A bribe?"

"You betcha."

"You know I rarely cook anymore."

"Then I can't help you. Goodbye, Mrs. Reynolds."

"I said I rarely cook anymore. But there just happens to be a fresh chess pie in my car."

Goetz stood, grabbing his coat. "Let's go. Time's a-wastin'."

It was all I could do to keep up with him rushing out of the police building.

17

"Where's your hearing aid?" asked Goetz in between bites of the chess pie. It was a good thing I had brought paper plates and forks.

We were sitting in my car parked on a side street.

"I got a new one," I replied, lifting my hair. "See, you can hardly tell I have one. It's nude and tiny. Fits right into the ear."

"No GPS anymore?"

"I know you all thought that was pretty funny keeping tabs on me, but it was a real invasion of privacy."

"I seem to remember that it saved your life . . . that little GPS device."

"I don't want to talk about it," I said, suddenly remembering Jake. I didn't want to think about him.

"You didn't make this pie, did you?" accused Goetz, tired of talking about the hearing aid.

Damn! I was caught. "How can you tell?"

"Cooking is just like fingerprints. Everyone has his or her own signature. The crust is different from other pies of yours."

"I paid Miss Eunice twenty dollars to make it," I confessed. "I don't enjoy cooking anymore. Takes too much out of me."

Goetz put down his fork and scrutinized me. "Are you depressed or something?"

"I don't know what it is. I've just got the blahs. I need to stick my nose into something interesting. Everything has been too calm lately."

"So you are seeking a solution to a mystery that does not exist."

I shrugged my shoulders.

"There is a name for people like you. Adrenaline junkies. You need a rush of excitement juice."

"I do my exercises, go to doctor appointments, and then the rest of the day is free. Miss Eunice, who is practically perfect in almost every way, oversees the house and the business. I just run errands now and then. Everything on the farm is caught up. Charles handles the employees for me so there is really nothing for me to do but get into other people's business. I feel . . . useless." My eyes teared up.

"Is the irrepressible Josiah Reynolds gonna cry?"

I started to bawl my eyes out for real. Goetz could be such a hard-ass when he wanted to be.

"Hey, is this for real? Come on now. I didn't mean to make you cry."

I sobbed out loud.

"Stop it, Josiah. You don't know how lucky you are. You should be dead. Falling off a cliff and then having a maniac after you for years. You beat the odds. You should be rejoicing." He handed me his handkerchief. "Please don't cry. Your life is good. You'll find your way. Just stop crying. I'm sorry. I shouldn't have teased you so."

My face perked up. "What was that?"

"I said I was sorry for being such a jerk. You're a good woman. That's why everyone comes to you when they're in trouble."

My intro at last. "Speaking of trouble, there is someone I want you to check out," I confessed while dabbing my eyes.

Goetz leaned back in the car seat. "I should have known the tears were a con."

"Don't you want to make it up to me? After all, I did go to the trouble of making a chess pie."

"Miss Eunice."

"Go to the trouble of having Miss Eunice make a chess pie for you."

"Can I keep the rest of the pie?"

"It has your name on it."

"What do you need?"

I gave Goetz a sincere smile for once.

18

I stopped by Mavis' house on the way home.

"Josiah, nice to see you again," declared Mavis, opening the screen door.

"Hope I'm not bothering you," I said, noticing that Mavis was still in her morning housecoat. It was the afternoon.

"You'll have to excuse me," she confided. "I don't feel like gussying up lately."

"I understand."

"Yes, you would, being a fellow widow and all. Please come in. Come in." She motioned to a chair, which was not littered with newspapers, baskets of laundry or dirty dishes. Mavis gave a sheepish grin. "No need to keep up with things now. Terry always favored a tidy house, but . . ."

I cut in. "I know, Mavis. Death throws you off your game. Give yourself time. You'll find your groove again."

"You understand. My daughter doesn't. She was on me this morning. She wants everything normal, but it's not, is it, Josiah?" Mavis looked about the room. "You know, I don't even see colors now. Everything is gray."

I reached over and patted her hand. There was no need to say anything, but I knew exactly what she meant about the lack of color. We both sat in our own thoughts and memories until I broke the silence. "Mavis, I was wondering how your dog is doing?"

"He's fine. The vet flushed out his stomach and he's right as rain."

"Did he eat something poisonous?"

"The vet thought he might have gotten into some insecticide, although I don't know how. We didn't have any in the house and don't have close neighbors. I've been wondering where he could have gotten hold of that stuff. Why do you ask?"

"You mentioned that his claws were bluish. It just clicked with something I read in an Agatha Christie book once." I thought for a moment. "Are you sure the vet thought your dog had been poisoned?"

"I wasn't at the vet. My daughter took him. She said they pumped out his stomach. Why?"

"How is your cat doing? Was he sick at any time?"

"No. He was never ill."

"Anybody visit before the dog got sick?"

"Well, Jean Louis paid Terry a visit, but that was all."

"How was Terry after the visit?"

"I don't understand the question. What are you aiming at?"

"Was he agitated or angry?"

"Not that I noticed, but Terry said he felt tired afterwards and he went to bed earlier than usual. He had his heart attack later that night."

"I see."

"What are you trying to say, Josiah?" asked Mavis becoming alarmed.

"Nothing," I assured. "Just being nosey. You know how I am. I like to know how all the pieces fit into the puzzle."

Mavis' face relaxed. "Yes, you have quite a reputation. You like puzzles, don't you? Speaking of puzzles, did you get a chance to study Terry's notebook?"

"Yes, I did," I replied, pulling the notebook from my pocket and handing it to her.

Mavis received it gratefully. "Anything?"

"Terry wrote some of it in code that I couldn't break, but from what I could detect, he wrote down notations of stolen paintings."

"From the Gardner Museum?"

"No. These were paintings stolen by the Nazis during World War II."

Mavis looked surprised.

"Did he ever mention that to you?"

"Never," she murmured. "You think you know everything about a person and then something like this pops up." She shook her head. "Goodness."

I stood up. "I hope your dog is fine."

"Oh, I hope so too. He's such a darling. I want him back. I hope my daughter doesn't get too attached to him."

I nodded. "Oh, look. There's a pen on the floor." I bent over precariously and picked up the pen and a little fuzz ball of dog hair and a partial dog nail along with it. The dog must have chewed on his paws. I handed Mavis the pen while hiding the fuzz ball in my palm.

Mavis saw me to the door and watched as I hobbled down her stoop and finally into my car.

I headed home with the ball of dog hair in my coat pocket.

19

I went to the diagnostic lab where I'd had a slab of chocolate tested following a friend's death earlier in the year. I asked for Charlotte.

"Mrs. Reynolds!" exclaimed Charlotte as soon as she saw me.

"Hi. How have you been doing?"

"Fine, but my boyfriend left me."

"Oh, no."

She gave me a cheeky grin. "He caught me with his professor."

"NO!" (Hadn't I surmised that?)

"I still can't figure how he found out."

"His loss."

"Actually, I'm happier."

"That's all that matters."

"What brings you here? Another case?"

I pulled out a little ball of fur from a plastic bag.

Charlotte looked at it curiously.

"Can you test for cyanide poisoning from fur or a partial nail?"

Charlotte's smile exploded. "Cyanide is usually tested through the blood, but yes, Mrs. Reynolds. Yes, we can try." She then gave me a salacious grin.

I grinned back.

20

June was taking a bubble bath when I popped my head into her sumptuous marble bathroom.

"Make sure those bubbles hide all your nasty old lady bits," I teased.

"Always a pleasure to see you too, Josiah."

"Are you being sarcastic?" I asked, sipping out of the champagne glass that had been sitting on the bathtub ledge. "How do you get out of that thing anyway?" Her bath was a deep soaking tub. I sat on its edge.

June reached for her glass, but I held it out of her reach and drained it.

"Get me a new glass, if you don't mind," demanded June, scowling. "I don't like drinking after people and why the hell are you bothering me? Can't a woman take a bath in peace? Next you'll be coming in while I'm on the toilet."

Looking about the room, I spied another champagne glass and a bottle on the sink counter. "Why do you already have another glass in here?" Then it dawned on me. "Oh goodness, you weren't expecting someone, were you?"

Just then I heard the unmistakable voice of a man in June's bedroom.

"Are you decent, my little bubala?" A giggle. "I hope not. Here I come. Ready or not."

The bathroom door opened and in stuck a head, hoping for a naughty glimpse of the eighty-eight-year-old mistress of the house. Instead, he saw me sitting on the edge of the bathtub holding a champagne glass staring back.

"What's up, Buttercup?" I greeted.

"We've been caught red-handed, my boy. The jig is up," quipped June, struggling to get out of the tub.

As I passed Liam, I handed him my glass. "Oh, Liam, take care. Her bones are brittle," I whispered.

"Yes, ma'am."

Before closing the door, I saluted June.

She returned a toothy grin, knowing that her secret was safe.

I mean, who would believe it!

21

The doorbell rang.

Old habits die hard.

Most people would immediately answer the door, but I went to a side room where the security monitors were located. I moved the joystick on the camera to get a visual ID.

Even with Baby hovering by my side, my heart sped up as I placed my hand on the door handle. My breathing quickened.

"Are you going to open the door?" asked Eunice, coming up behind me. "It's Detective Goetz. I looked out the window." Knowing that I still panicked when anyone came to the house, she gently moved me out of the way and opened the door. "Good morning," she said.

"Good morning, Miss Eunice. Is the mistress of the house around? I've got something for her."

"She's right here. Come on in. We were just working on getting the house right. There's a tour coming in a few hours."

Goetz stepped inside the door. Seeing me, he held up a manila envelope. "I'll only keep her for a few minutes, I promise."

"Let's go to my office," I offered. "We're almost finished anyway."

"How's business?" asked Goetz, looking around.

"We are booked into next year," announced Eunice proudly. "We could be booked every weekend, but I'm only allowed two Saturdays out of the month for receptions plus one tour every two weeks now."

"The Butterfly is my home," I cautioned. "A private residence."

"We could make a fortune, but she won't let us," laughed Eunice, "but you didn't come here to hear me complain about Josiah's lack of business sense. I'll be in the kitchen. Nice to see you again, Detective."

"Same here."

Goetz followed me into my office, but couldn't close the door as Baby took up residence on its threshold. "How do you get this dog to move?" he asked, trying to shut the door.

"You don't. He basically does as he pleases."

"I see." Goetz turned and tossed the envelope on my desk.

I opened it and perused the contents. "There's not much here."

"The guy is clean. At least in the States."

"Can't you check with Interpol?"

"I have no valid reason to check up on this guy. If I get caught using more of the Department's resources without cause, I could get into trouble. I am months away from retirement. I'm not going to jeopardize that because your nose is twitching."

"You could have called me with this."

"Maybe I wanted to see you."

"You've seen me."

Goetz tilted his head. "You're a hard woman to get to know up close and personal."

"Maybe I don't want you to get up close and personal."

"You could do worse and have," Goetz ran on. "You're batty about old movies, right? *Gilda* with Rita Hayworth is playing at the Kentucky Theater tomorrow night. I'll pick you up at six. Wear something pretty."

I meant to say "no thank you", but heard something that sounded like, "all right," come out of my mouth. Who said that?

I don't like men who try to dominate me. I like to be in control, so why did I agree to this date against my better judgment?

Why indeed?

22

Goetz showed up a little before six. He was freshly shaved, bushy eyebrows trimmed, nails manicured, hair cut, shirt pressed, and smelling of expensive men's cologne.

I didn't look bad myself wearing a pale green silk tunic, which accented my green eyes and highlighted my red hair.

We both surveyed each other with unexpected approval.

Before leaving, I let the Kitty Kaboodle Gang inside and set the alarm, promising Baby that I would bring home a treat for him.

Goetz opened the car door and helped me settle in with my wrap and purse. Satisfied that I was buckled in properly, he shut the car door and got in himself.

"Were you that courteous with your wife?"

"No, but I don't intend to make the same mistake again."

I didn't know how to respond so I stared out the window, mentally reciting lines from *Gilda*.

Rita Hayworth as Gilda: *You do hate me, don't you, Johnny?*
Glenn Ford as Johnny Farrell: *I don't think you have any idea of how much.*
Rita Hayworth: *Hate is a very exciting emotion. Haven't you noticed? Very exciting. I hate you too, Johnny. I hate you so much I think I'm going to die from it. Darling . . . I think I'm going to die from it.*

As I rode along, I wondered where this relationship with Goetz was going. I didn't even know his first name. I don't remember him ever telling me. But one thing was for sure . . . I was never going to say to him, "I hate you so much I think I'm going to die from it. Darling . . . I think I'm going to die from it."

23

The next day I got a call from Charlotte.

"Mrs. Reynolds?"

"Yes, Charlotte. Did you find anything?"

"The tests were inconclusive. I can't tell you that the fur or the nails tested positive for cyanide. I'm sorry."

Disappointed, I replied, "I'm sorry too. There goes my theory."

"Is there any other test you want me to try?"

"No. Thanks for trying."

"Anytime, Mrs. Reynolds."

"Goodbye." I hung up.

Darn! Where do I go from here?

24

I needed concrete evidence, which meant I had to look for it. That meant I had to snoop. In order to snoop I had to get into June's house without arousing suspicions about my being there, so I made up the story that my septic tank had backed up.

Of course, June said I could stay with her until it was fixed. She put me in an ugly bedroom in the guest wing of the house, making for a longer walk to the elevator since I wouldn't use the staircase with my bum leg. Guess her Ladyship was annoyed with me for cutting into her whoopee party the other day.

The first night, Jean Louis stayed up very late working on the portrait. I finally fell asleep waiting for him to leave and missed my chance. The second night, he and Lady Elsmere went to a dinner party at some "swell's" house on Old Frankfort Pike.

I watched from the upstairs window as the Bentley traveled down the long driveway and turned onto Tates Creek Road. Satisfied, I hurried to the elevator and pressed the first-floor button.

It didn't move.

I pressed again.

It didn't budge. Didn't make a humming sound. Didn't do a thing!

Hells Bells! It seemed that someone wanted to keep me upstairs for the night. Someone had turned off the elevator!

No one in this house would do that. That elevator was for the convenience of Lady Elsmere. It even had a backup system if the electricity was cut off. One had to have a key to lock up the elevator and Charles kept all the keys downstairs in his office. No one in this house would dare to turn off the elevator. No one.

No one except maybe Jean Louis.

I exited the elevator and looked wistfully at the curving staircase. My heart began pounding against my chest, but I had no other choice. I had to make it down that staircase.

After wiping moist hands on my pants, I began the descent down the stairs. Clinging to the banister, I took one step at a time. Sweat broke out on my brow, but I continued until I finally reached the ground floor.

It had taken me a good ten minutes to carefully climb down the master staircase.

Unsteadily I made my way to the library where Jean Louis kept his paintings. The door was locked.

But I was prepared for that. I had gone into Charles' office yesterday and unlocked the safe where Charles kept a second set of keys for the house.

How did I know the combination? I was to be an executor of June's will if something should happen to Charles before she died.

Bet Jean Louis didn't know that little bit of info.

I wish I had had the forethought to take the extra elevator key at that time.

I unlocked the door to the library and turned on the light. I looked at the antique grandfather clock in the corner. Twenty-five minutes had passed since my descent to the ground floor. I breathed a sigh of relief. I had plenty of time still.

June and Jean Louis would be gone for hours.

Feeling moisture on my upper lip, I wiped it off with the back of my hand. Pulling some books out from their shelf, I unearthed a small digital camera where I had hidden it yesterday while Jean Louis was on a bathroom break.

Catching my reflection in an antique mirror, I looked like the Cheshire Cat. I started humming the *Pink Panther* theme song.

I pulled out two small paintings from Jean Louis' collection and began photographing them from all angles. Then I turned the paintings over and photographed the backs and sides of the canvases in detail. With a small knife, I scraped off a few flakes of paint and cut a tiny piece of canvas from each painting, putting the scrapes into little plastic tubes that florists use to water cut flowers. Placing the paintings back exactly as I found them, I began photographing a larger canvas when I heard the Bentley.

I shot a glance at the clock. Only an hour had passed since I entered the library. It was too early for them to be home. But the smooth purr of the Bentley was unmistakable.

My heart was pounding as I put the painting back. I stuck the tubes behind some books and the camera in my pants pocket before I turned off the light and locked the library door.

The back door opened and I heard June say, "I didn't see a light on in the library. Are you sure you had turned it off?"

Oh crap!

Crossing the hallway, I rushed into the formal parlor and made my way in the dark to the dining room and then to the west wing as heavy footsteps sounded on the marble hallway going in the opposite direction from me. I turned left and found the servants' staircase and bounded up as fast as I could. It's funny how adrenaline can really give a person that extra energy to get her caboose going.

"Darn it. There's something wrong with the elevator," June uttered in consternation. "Jean Louis, can you go upstairs and see what the matter is. Maybe it's stuck."

The echo of Jean Louis bounding up the staircase gave me chills. How could that fat pudgy elf move so quickly?

I would never make it to my room in time. Shouldering a wall, I melted in with the shadows and kept moving until I felt a doorknob. I gave it a turn until the door opened. Silently I entered an empty bedroom and kept the door open just enough to see down the hallway toward the elevator.

I watched Jean Louis surreptitiously glance down both hallways before stepping into the elevator. "Here's the problem," he called out. "The ON switch has been turned off." After a few seconds, the elevator returned to life. It began to descend to the ground floor.

"I bet Josiah turned it off accidentally," June yelled up the staircase.

Seeing my chance, I stepped out from the guestroom and turned on the hall lights. Leaning over the balustrade I blurted, "Someone say my name?"

The elevator reached the ground floor with a shudder as Jean Louis stepped out. Both he and June looked up.

"The elevator wasn't working," accused June.

"It seems to be working now. You guys are home early."

"Jean Louis started feeling ill, so we came home."

"Did you happen to be in the library a few moments ago?" asked Jean Louis. "I thought I saw a light coming from the room as we drove up."

"Nope. Was in my room reading when I heard the car. Are you feeling better, Jean Louis? You don't seem ill."

Waving his hands with a theatrical flourish, Jean Louis replied, "A mild headache. Nothing to worry about."

"I'm not worried, Jean Louis."

Jean Louis' eyes narrowed.

I motioned to June. "If Jean Louis has a headache, he will surely want to go to his guesthouse. Come on up, June. You can tell me all about the party."

June bid Jean Louis good night as he kissed her gloved hand. She beamed with pleasure.

Jean Louis gave me another spiteful glance before taking his leave.

I threw him a kiss.

He blanched.

Gee, if looks could kill.

I seemed to have a knack for pissing him off.

I guess it was a gift.

25

After listening to June chatter for over an hour about the dinner party, I finally got her to bed.

I was worn out. Glad to get to bed myself, I hurried down the hallway to my room.

I should have been alert. I really should have. I really, really should have. But I felt safe.

The lights were out in my room when I opened the door. "That's funny," I said to myself. "I thought I left them on."

That's when I sensed someone behind me and heard a whoosh sound.

Then *my* lights went out.

26

I remember only bits and pieces. I remember flashes of crawling. I remember struggling for my cell phone, but it was out of reach on a table. I remember pushing the table over.

I remember pushing a number on the phone. I remember saying the name Goetz. I remember hearing a siren.

But that's all.

27

Someone shook my shoulder and said, "Sleeping Beauty's awake."

"Let me take a look at her." Someone shoved a light in my face. "Follow the light, please." Then it was, "Can you feel this?"

"Where am I?" I asked.

"In the emergency room."

"Goetz?"

"Yeah."

"Why are you here?"

"You called me."

"Hey, that hurts," I snapped at the doctor.

"Only been conscious for a few seconds and already bitching. Seems normal. Can I take her home now, Doc?"

"Yes, but someone needs to stay with her. If she vomits or feels dizzy, bring her back in."

Goetz groused, "Sounds like a fun night."

"What happened?" I asked as Goetz put a coat around my shoulders.

"Someone rang your bell."

"Huh?"

"Tapped you on the head. Remember anything?"

I shook my head. "Ow, that hurts," I cried, holding my head. There was a bandage on the back of my skull.

"So don't shake your head."

"You're all sympathetic."

"I was just settling in for the night with a roast beef sandwich and my favorite TV show when you called."

"I called?"

"You said my name and then the phone went dead."

"Oh."

"I first went to your house and couldn't find you, but that dog of yours ran up to Lady Elsmere's house, so I followed. Otherwise, I wouldn't have found you."

"Baby?"

"He's okay. He's with a woman named Bess. Oh, by the way, you're going to have to get a new lock on your front door."

"Why?"

"I shot the lock off." Goetz hesitated for a few seconds. "You might need a new front door as well."

"Let me guess. You kicked in the door."

Goetz shrugged.

"My knight in shining armor."

Goetz's face morphed into a look of annoyance, then brightened when he realized that I was being serious.

"How many women can say that a man shot and kicked in a door to save them. Quite sexy, reeeallleee," I murmured, dozing off.

Goetz shook me. "I doubt you will feel that way when you see the mess. Come on. Let's get you home. I have to babysit you for the next twelve hours."

"What about work?"

"I called in. I'm taking a personal day."

But I didn't hear Goetz as I had fallen asleep.

Goetz checked the time on his watch. He put my purse in my lap and held onto the back of my coat as he wheeled me out of the waiting room.

Goetz seemed placid and almost serene but there was no mistaking the anger emanating from his eyes. He was going to find out who did this and beat the stuffing out of him . . . or as we say in the South . . . horsewhip him . . . or in less genteel circles . . . whup his ass.

28

I awoke to the sound of whining. It took a while to rotate my stiff neck toward the source of the irritating sound.

It was Baby trying to jiggle the mattress with his head. When he saw my opened eyes, his tail pounded a delighted dance upon the floor.

This thumping did nothing to encourage the cats, either lying on my chest or along both sides of me, to move. I was covered in a furry shroud. They blinked their sleepy eyes as I shooed them, remaining in their comfortable positions.

Baby licked my hand.

"What time is it?" I glanced at my old-fashioned radio clock. It was the afternoon.

Pushing the cats off, I sat up and swung my legs over the side of the bed. Sitting for a moment, I reassessed my condition. I didn't feel nauseous or dizzy or even constipated. That was always a plus . . . not feeling constipated.

My landline phone was still on the nightstand.

So far so good.

Making sure the bedroom door was closed first, I dialed the number.

One ring.

Someone picked up on the other end.

I whispered, "Rosebud."

A click sounded, ending the call. The person on the other end had hung up.

Somehow, somewhere, someone would get a message to my daughter.

And it would not be traced by anyone, as it was under the radar of modern technology.

Sometimes the old ways are the best.

29

There was a knock on the door. "Are you decent?"

"Who, me? Yeah, I'm decent."

Goetz opened the door and walked in. "The doc called and said your scans were fine. If you feel all right, I'd like to leave. Got things to do."

I was glad Goetz was going home. "No problem." I followed him to the front door, which apparently had been repaired during my slumber. "Thank you for all your help." I was about to close the door.

He turned, facing me. "What's the problem? Not good looking enough for you?"

"Excuse me?"

"I've done everything but do cartwheels for you, lady, and I'm getting nowhere."

"I don't know what you mean?"

"You know damn well what I mean. There's no sizzle, no juice from you."

"You want juice? Go to a juice bar."

"You owe me."

"I don't owe you a thing."

Goetz shook his head. "If you only knew."

"I just got conked on the head and knocked out. How sexy can I be, you jerk? Is that why you've helped me through this? Thought I was gonna come out in a skimpy nighty and say, 'Hey, Mister Policeman, thanks so much for helping little old me. Show me your nightstick!'"

"I'll show you something," growled Goetz. Grabbing me, he enveloped me in his thick arms and tilted my head back.

I pushed against him. "Let go," I demanded. "You're a pig."

"Shut up," whispered Goetz. "You talk too much." His lips pressed against mine.

I started to struggle but his grip was like iron . . . and then I stopped. Goetz smelled like the ocean, big and expansive, and full of life. I don't know why the ocean smells like that, but it does.

Jake had always reminded me of the woods. He smelled of moss, trees, and dark, rich earth. But Goetz was the ocean. I felt my feet in hot sand and heard the crashing of the waves.

Suddenly Goetz pushed me away.

I jerked my eyes open and there standing in front of us was Eunice with an amused smile on her face.

"She's all yours," seethed Goetz as he bounded to his car.

"Someone's got a bee in his bonnet today," remarked Eunice before trotting into the Butterfly.

Watching Goetz leave, I was very, very confused.

30

"You're not going to sue, are you, Josiah?" inquired June before sipping her tea.

We were seated in the library before a roaring fire.

"I don't think so, but a bauble or two might make me happy," I replied, eying the ruby and diamond leopard pin climbing down her left shoulder.

"Can't you wait until I'm dead to get some of your little baubles? You know which jewelry I'm leaving you."

"Why wait?" I replied.

Jean Louis snickered before biting into an English tea biscuit.

"I still don't understand what happened," June pouted.

"I told you. I slipped and as I was falling, I must have

hit my head against the wall and checked out for a while," I fibbed. I tried not to snarl at Jean Louis, who I think was the dirty rotten skunk who'd hit me.

"It all sounds rather curious to me," she sniffed, "but the important thing is that you are fine. It's just so strange that the elevator had been turned off, and then your fall. Yes, the whole matter is rather curious."

"Let's forget about it, shall we."

I could see that June sensed something about the story was fishy, but she decided to let it go. "If you say so."

"I do say so."

"Then I have something to announce," she preened.

"Oh dear. Now what," I muttered with a sloppy grin.

"Jean Louis has finished my portrait and it is sensational!"

I spooned honey into my hot tea. "That's great. Congratulations, Jean Louis." It was all I could do not to reach over and slap his smug face.

"Merci. I have finished a masterpiece for a great lady and now it is time for me to go home."

Alarmed, I almost dropped my tea. "You can't do that!" I blurted out.

Both Jean Louis and June looked startled at my outburst.

"I mean, June . . . you should give Jean Louis a big sendoff . . . a ball. That way you could show off the portrait to everyone. It would be its grand introduction into the world. You could invite all the art and horse people. You haven't had a formal ball for so long. It would be wonderful."

Jean Louis fluttered his pudgy little hands. "No. No. I have intruded on Lady Elsmere's good graces for too long. I have finished my little masterpiece. Now I go home. No ball. No ball, please."

"I won't hear of you leaving yet, Jean Louis. In fact, I think the ball is a wonderful idea. And I'm going to hold up signing your check until the night of the ball, so you will have to stay."

Jean Louis gave June a nasty look before he mastered his emotions. It was only a split second, but I caught it. "Then you hold me hostage. No money. I will have to stay until I collect, n'est-ce pas?"

June's wrinkled face beamed with joy. "Then it is settled. When shall we have it, Josiah?"

I quickly tabulated how much time I needed . . . but not for a ball. "We can't keep Jean Louis too much longer, but this weekend is too quick. How about Saturday after next?"

"That soon? I can't put on a ball that quickly."

"I have a life, Madame. I need to get back to it," pleaded Jean Louis. "Maybe I leave and then come back for the ball."

"I'll compromise, Jean Louis. Just stay a few more days and I'll throw a cocktail party. We'll serve champagne and hors d'oeuvres. Plenty of chocolate. Everyone can see the painting. Then you can take a night flight."

"But what about the ball?" I whined. A few days simply would not give me enough time to set things up on my end.

"We can't keep this genius in Kentucky that long." She turned to Jean Louis. "It's selfish of me to intrude so on your time, but it would mean so much to me, Jean Louis . . . and I am paying you a lot of money."

"I would love it better if you paid in cash," joked Jean Louis.

We all twittered at that suggestion.

"Now that it is settled that Jean Louis is staying for a few more days, I'm going upstairs to gather my things," I announced while putting down my teacup.

"Bess has your things in the kitchen," said June. "She also has a pie for you to take home."

"Then I'll just look around in my room to make sure she has everything," I chirped as I rose.

"I'll go with you to help," Jean Louis suggested, getting up from his chair.

I swung around like a barnyard cat ready for a fight. "I don't need your help!"

"Josiah!" gasped June.

"I mean, thank you, but no. I need to do this alone. I need to be more independent. Face those demons by myself."

"I just thought you might need assistance. You don't want to have another accident," preached Jean Louis, looking smug again. He gave June a knowing glance.

Oh, how I wanted to slap his face! I knew he was the one who had knocked me out. I hated his pretentious bloated face with his beady little rat's eyes glaring at me.

"I'll be all right. But thank you for trying to help. You stay here and enjoy your tea with June. I'll say my goodbyes now." I kissed June on the cheek and left the room.

I hurried up to the second floor in the elevator. Once out in the hallway, I leaned over the banister to make sure Jean Louis hadn't followed.

He hadn't. I could still hear him talking to June in the library, which is why I had left the door open.

Good. I hobbled into the bedroom where I had taken refuge on that night. I silently closed the door trying to ignore that my left leg was hurting like the dickens. The doctor had put me on new pain medication. Obviously it wasn't working. Maybe when I got home, I would medicate myself from my private stash of contraband . . . that is if I could even bend to get into the floor safe. *I'm going to have to get a wall safe*, I thought to myself. Another thought popped into my head. *Concentrate. Concentrate on the task at hand.*

Going over to an eighteenth century writing desk, I took out a drawer and then pushed on a tab under the desk.

A secret panel popped open.

Reaching into it, I pulled out my camera and put it into the pocket of my jacket. Opening the door just a bit, I peeked into the hallway. Seeing no one, I quickly limped down the servants' staircase.

Carefully negotiating the stairs, I made my way into the kitchen. "Hey, Bess," I said. "I hear you have a pie with my name on it."

"Find anything upstairs?"

I turned to find Jean Louis sitting at the kitchen table having a piece of pie with a cup of coffee. "I thought you were having tea with June. Wow, a piece of pie after afternoon tea."

He patted his belly. "Got to keep my weight up." He took a sip of coffee.

I turned to Bess. "Help me out with my bag?"

Bess gave Jean Louis a sideways glance. "Sure. You get your pie. It's in the fridge."

I hurried to retrieve my pie and followed Bess out to my golf cart.

Jean Louis followed us. "Josiah, would you mind dropping me off at the guest house?"

Bess stepped forward, grabbing the pie out of my hands. "I'm afraid you might jostle the pie on the way home. You're so clumsy." She got in the front seat, holding the pie in her lap. "Mr. Jean Louis, you get in the back and we'll drop you off."

Puffing, Jean Louis had no recourse but to get in the back of my golf cart. This was not the way it was supposed to go. He silently brooded as we parted ways at the guesthouse.

Once out of earshot, Bess laughed out loud. "That's one hair-raising Frenchman. Oooh, he gives me the shivers."

I laughed as well. Bess was one smart cookie.

"Let me off here."

I slowed the cart and Bess hopped out.

She placed the pie on the floor of the cart. "You don't think I believe that cock-and-bull story about you tripping, do you?"

"What do you think happened, Bess?"

"I think Jean Louis rapped you upside your head."

"That's what I think too."

"Why don't you tell Miss June, then?"

"I don't think she would believe me. She is under the spell of Monsieur Jean Louis. Besides, I need some time. I don't want to confront him yet. Keep this mum, will ya?"

"I'll have Liam keep an eye on our guest."

"Liam? Isn't he too busy belting down June's bourbon?"

"I guess he needs a few snorts to put up with Miss June."

"So you know about that?"

"Liam's a big boy and knows what he's doing. He's in his fifties, after all."

"Still."

"Actually, Liam's having a great time and Miss June is giddy with the attention, but this May/December fling won't last too much longer."

"Have you ever seen an old lady with such a sex drive?"

"It beats the rocking chair . . . or the grave. Most old folks give up, but not Miss June. You gotta give her credit. Don't worry about them. They're both of age and know the facts of life."

Hmmm. The facts of life.

Maybe I should rethink some things.

31

Goetz opened his door.

"Why do I owe you?"

"Jeez."

"No, tell me. You said I owed you. That has been bothering me. Why do I owe you? I know you're not dumb enough to think that helping me with a concussion one night deserves favors."

I walked past him into his apartment. It was actually quite nice, with Mission Arts and Crafts furniture. I looked closer. I was beginning to doubt the pieces were reproductions, but the real McCoy.

"You're the only woman I know that would come to a man's apartment to chew him out and then get sidetracked by some sticks of wood."

I shrugged. "I'm not finished yelling. I would really like an answer to my question, but I also want to know where you got this collection."

Goetz grabbed me by the shoulders and shook. When he saw that my eyes hadn't rolled back in my head yet, he shook again and harder.

"Can't you see that I'm crazy about you? Have been since the first time we met."

I pushed him off. "Yeah, I love the way you show it. Don't you ever touch me like that again! I am tired of men thinking that they can do what they want to me and suffer no consequences. I swear that the next man who puts his hands on me is going to get a bullet in the leg."

"I was trying to shake some sense into you." He fell onto his couch and threw up his hands in defeat. "I can never catch a break with you. First, it was the death of Richard Pidgeon. I knew you had nothing to do with it. I tried to persuade my Captain that we were going down the wrong path . . . that it was death by misadventure, but he said that he would follow O'nan's lead."

"Is that why you tried to plant a listening device on me and ransack my house during a search?"

"I know that it is hard for rich people like you to understand average working Joes like me, but even for you, I was not going to be put on suspension and lose everything I had worked for."

"Rich people like me?" I sneered. "I hope you don't think I have lots of money. The fact is I have my retirement fund and that's about all. The settlement I got from the city has been spent on medical bills, and the little revenue I get from the farm goes back into the farm. I have very little money myself. And I have worked hard all my life too, buddy. Nobody gave me handouts. What I've got, I earned."

Goetz lifted up his craggy face. "You want a beer? I'm tired of fighting."

I plopped down beside him. "I am too. We're too old to argue like this anyway."

"You wear me out, Josiah."

"What do you want, Goetz?"

"I want to go to the movies with someone. I want to be able to call at ten o'clock at night and tell someone about my day. I want someone to buy a birthday card for. I'm tired of being alone every single night."

I placed my hand on top of his big catcher's mitt of a hand. "We can be friends, Goetz. You can call me late at night. I'll go to the movies with you."

"You know what I mean?"

"Sure, I get lonely too. And it will get better when you retire. You can visit your grandkids more often then."

Goetz leaned toward me. "I've got a secret. I hate kids. All that screaming and neediness. Kids suck you dry."

I laughed.

"That's nice."

"What is?"

"Your laugh. You've got a nice laugh."

"Thank you."

"Let's go to dinner. I'm starving."

"You paying?"

"Yeah."

"What are we waiting for then?"

As we were going out the door, I asked, "You never did answer my question."

"What question?"

"How do I owe you?"

"Be quiet, woman, I was just baiting you. Let it go. "

Somehow I didn't believe him. There was something still unspoken. A deep secret between us. I could feel it.

32

The phone rang.

I lifted the receiver from its cradle. "Hello," I said, groggily looking at the radio clock. It was two in the morning.

"Josiah, this is Mavis Bailey."

"Mavis? Why are you whispering?"

"Someone is trying to break into the house. Help me!"

"Mavis, hang up and call the police."

"There's someone in the living room."

"Lock your bedroom door. Mavis, hang up and call the police! Mavis! Mavis!"

A blood-curdling scream sounded on the phone.

"MAVIS! MAVIS!"

The phone went dead.

33

I got to Mavis' house before the police, but I heard sirens in the distance. They couldn't be too far away. All the lights in the house were off. Knocking on the front door, I tried to push it open. It was locked. "Mavis! Mavis! It's Josiah Reynolds. Open up!"

Nothing.

Taking a flashlight, I went to the back of the house.

The glass on the back door had been broken and the door stood open.

I pulled a stun gun out of my pocket while I pushed the door open wider with my foot. I didn't know if someone like a deranged druggie was still in the house, but I didn't want to wait for the cops. Seconds might count.

Reaching around the doorjamb, I felt for a light switch. The room flooded with bright light.

"MAVIS!" Hearing nothing, I stepped into the kitchen, avoiding the broken glass. "I've got a gun. If you're still here, go out the front. The cops are coming." I listened but the house was silent. No running footsteps.

Feeling braver, I kept turning on more lights and searching for Mavis. The sirens kept getting louder. When were the police going to get here?

Finally, I turned on the hall light and saw an arm outstretched from the bedroom. "Mavis?" Throwing caution to the wind I ran down the hall.

Mavis was in her nightgown, lying on the floor. Her lips were bloodied. "Oh, Mavis," I gushed, bending down. I checked her pulse. It was faint.

"Help me up," she whispered. "Help me." She began struggling.

"Mavis. Let me support you, but I really don't think you should stand. The police are almost here."

"You. YOU!" she hissed. She raised her arm and pointed to the corner of the bedroom.

"What is it?" I asked, half-expecting to see someone hiding in the corner. But there was no one there.

"It's Mama!" she cried. "MAMA'S HERE!"

The hair on the back of my neck stood on end as I dragged Mavis out of the bedroom.

34

Okay. Call me crazy . . . thinking I could cheat death by dragging Mavis out of her bedroom. Did I think Cordelia Sharp was back from the grave and coming for her daughter? You betcha.

Do I believe that ghosts are real? Not on your life.

I just know that the rolling hills of Kentucky are rife with the dead waiting to interfere with the living. The dark, rich earth of Kentucky is saturated with the blood and bones of Native American warriors, frontiersmen and women, boys from the North and South, victims of blood feuds and tobacco wars, murdered slaves, drug runners, and countless luckless women who loved the wrong men.

This land is old and the hate in the soil is strong and cries out for vengeance.

People are always seeing haints, but few will say they believe in ghosts as it defies science or God. But there is nothing scientific or holy in being haunted. It's a damnable thing to have happen to you.

I know Kentucky. She's a beautiful mistress that turns on you. She will lure you to your death if you don't keep a steady eye on her. Will it be death on the palisades, a coal mine explosion, falling off a horse, drowning in Kentucky's many lakes or rivers, or bloodshed by one of her sons?

She has a long, long history of violence at the hands of her sons and daughters. It's bred in us.

Kentuckians are charming, friendly, and hospitable, but never, never double-cross us or harm one of our kin. We can be vicious. Even the dead.

Kentucky is not called the dark and bloody ground for nothing.

Dragging Canoe, chief of the Cherokees, warned Daniel Boone, "We have given you a fine land, Brother, but you will find it under a cloud and a dark and bloody land."

Most people think Kentucky was always uninhabited. It was by the time Daniel Boone walked the Wilderness Trail, which is the most famous footpath in America, but historical records show that many peoples resided in Kentucky for thousands of years.

In fact, the last known Shawnee town near Lexington was Eskippakithiki, but when Daniel Boone reached its location, the town had been burned to the ground. Presumably, European diseases had decimated the local population so the surviving Shawnee relocated north of the Ohio River. Or at least, it is thought so.

Kentucky is old. The rocks are old. She was here long before the dinosaurs, before the Mastodon or Saber Tooth Tiger, before the Ice Age. Her earth is rich and dark with the sacrifices of many.

William S. Burroughs is quoted as saying, "America is not a young land. It is old and dirty and evil before the settlers, before the Indians. The evil is there waiting."

He might as well have said that about Kentucky.

The earliest stories of haints and strange beings begin with the Native Americans. They would tell the early fur trappers stories of other-worldly beings that had lived in or visited Kentucky.

And there was proof to back up the stories.

Pre-Columbian mummies with red hair have been found in our caves, including the Grand Daddy of them all–Mammoth Cave.

A Thomas Ashe writes of underground chambers below Lexington in his 1806 book, *Travels In America.* He claimed that a very large chamber with mummies having red hair had been discovered in 1783.

The Native Americans claimed that the mummies were not their people, but a forgotten race that had died out long ago.

There are records of these finds, but no one can actually locate the mummies now. One called "Fawn Hoof" was taken to the Smithsonian Institution in 1876 and discarded after she was dissected. However, a photograph of "Fawn Hoof" does survive.

Explorer Alonzo Alvarez de Pineda in 1519 wrote that he had encountered giants on the Mississippi River.

In 1965, a nine-foot tall skeleton was unearthed in Holly Creek, Kentucky. It supposedly had slits for eyes and nose rather than the normal round holes humans have. It was reburied by its finder, who took the whereabouts of the giant skeleton with him, but not before witnesses saw the remains.

Strange things happen in Kentucky. Always have. Always will.

Ghosts are seen in Whitehall, the home of Cassius M. Clay. Clay was a wealthy man who lived south of Lexington. He was a distant cousin of Henry Clay, the Great Compromiser. While Henry Clay was an entrenched slave owner, Cassius had his office several streets from Henry Clay's and wrote a fiery emancipationist newsletter.

Clay donated land to establish Berea College, which educated all races equally until the Jim Crow law called the Day Law was voted in by the Kentucky legislature.

While Cassius Clay is considered a person before his time, he had a dark side. Known as the Lion of Whitehall, Clay killed several men in duels and fights. He was also known for his love of the ladies. He married a fifteen-year-old girl when he was eighty-nine.

Whitehall, Clays' home, is considered very haunted. Visitors have reported seeing a woman in a nineteenth-century costume walking about, and many report feeling ill or anxious when the tour is about to reach the third floor of the house.

It is part of our folklore that the moment Cassius Clay died, a bolt of lightning decapitated the head of Henry Clay's monument in Lexington Cemetery.

The most haunted building in Kentucky is Bobby Mackey's Music World, located in Wilder across the river from Cincinnati. It is currently a country-western bar, but has in the past been an abattoir, a site for the Wilder Satanic group, and various nightclubs where multiple murders and suicides have occurred.

Even today patrons claim to hear and see other worldly events such as objects moving, a jukebox playing without electricity and even that spirits have attacked them. One patron sued Bobby Mackey's Music World claiming that a ghost in the restroom had assaulted him.

So . . . was I going to take precautions when Mavis said she was seeing her mother, Cordelia Sharp? If I could have dragged her out of the house I would have, but it was all I could do to get her into the living room. But Jumping Jehosaphat, what she said unnerved me!

35

Goetz caught a glimpse of himself in a store window. Stunned at what he saw, he stopped and stared. He didn't look like himself. Sure, he had dropped some weight and begun working out at the gym, more out of fear of a heart attack than any sense of vanity.

Behind him, women walking to work gave him a quick glance. Some gave him more than one.

He remembered what his daughter had said the last time he had seen her. She had laughed and said, "Daddy, you're turning into ugly sexy."

"What's that?"

"With men, there's pretty sexy and ugly sexy. Humphrey Bogart was ugly sexy. Pierce Brosnan is pretty sexy."

"Baby, you say the damnedest things."

She laughed again and kissed his cheek.

Goetz rubbed his cheek in remembrance of the kiss. He wondered if Josiah thought he was ugly sexy. She had never commented on his new muscular body or new clothes or whitened teeth.

The woman he had recently taken out on a date had. In fact, she had invited Goetz back to her place and Goetz had accepted.

Love the one you're with, right?

But she was not the woman he broke out into a sweat over.

That was Josiah.

But he just couldn't break the ice with her.

Goetz wanted so much to tell her that he had killed O'nan for her. Maybe then she would trust him. Give him a chance.

But then again, maybe not. She might turn him in. He couldn't take the chance.

How to unlock Josiah's heart? He couldn't find the key. So why did he want her?

Goetz recognized quality when he saw it and Josiah oozed it. He had even liked her when she was fat. Now sleek like a panther, he wondered if she was out of his league.

Goetz knew he was really just a broken-down hack parading in new duds. He looked at his reflection again. Who was he kidding?

How could a dame like Josiah fall for this run-down sack of goods? How indeed?

36

I was helping Eunice when the landline phone rang. Knowing that I still didn't like answering the phone, Eunice picked up the receiver. "Hello? Yes. This is Eunice. Yes, I can give her a message. Hmmm? Oh, that is terrible. I'm so sorry. Yes, I will tell her. Again, so sorry. Thank you for letting us know."

Eunice put the receiver back into its cradle, looking thoughtful.

"What is it, Eunice?" My heart was flipping flapjacks.

"That was Mavis Bailey's daughter. She said her mother died last night. Had a heart attack. Wanted you to know."

"Oh dear. That's terrible."

"Didn't you tell me that she saw her dead mother right after the police got there?"

"No. It was after I found her. She pointed and said that her mother was in the room."

Eunice shuddered. "The Bible says there are no such things as ghosts."

"Then whom did the Witch of Endor conjure up but the ghost of Samuel?"

"I keep forgetting that you were a professor of religious art," remarked Eunice.

"Nobody knows her Bible like a Southern Baptist girl."

"That's good because my church is having a Bible trivia game night. You are going to be in my group."

"What's in for me?"

"A cheap trophy and my eternal gratitude."

"How can I resist such a winning combination?"

Eunice grinned. "I know I can win if I have you."

"Pride goeth before a fall," I cautioned.

"Actually, it is 'pride goeth before destruction. And a haughty spirit before a fall.' "

"Point taken."

"But I sure would like to win. Yes, I sure would like to win."

I thought there may be more to this winning than the desire for a cheap trophy, but decided against questioning Eunice further.

Goetz was on his way over.

It was almost time for Lady Elsmere's party!

37

"I feel stupid in this," complained Goetz of his costume.

"You can't back out now. You promised to help," I reminded. "Here, help me with this zipper."

Goetz smiled. "Gladly."

"This new fondness for me is unnerving. Can't we go back to you hating me?"

"I never hated you."

"You sure acted like I was a pest."

"You are a pest."

"Oh, shut up."

"Quit squirming or this zipper is going to stay stuck. Ahhhh. There it goes."

"Thanks." I turned to face Goetz. "Now, let me inspect you."

Goetz was in a dark suit, holding a green apple and wearing a bowler hat.

"Are you supposed to be the man in the painting *The Son Of Man* by the Belgian surrealist Rene Magritte?"

Goetz shook his head. *"Thomas Crown Affair* with that other hot red-haired babe, Rene Russo."

"It's the same painting."

Goetz raised his eyebrows. "I didn't know it was a real painting. I did it because it was the easiest get-up I could wear. Who are you?"

I twirled around so he could see the dress. I had bought a cheap gold lamé dress and painted geometric eyes and squares on it. "I'm Adele Bloch, painted by Bauer Gustav Klimt."

"If you say so."

"I was going to be Dora Maar. She was the . . ."

"Mistress of Picasso. Yeah, I'm not completely stupid."

"I'm impressed."

"Why are we dressing up again?"

"I suggested it."

"Of course."

"It would keep Jean Louis busy if we were to have a costume party, dressing as a character from a painting. Being as vain as he is, I knew it would keep him occupied, as his costume would have to be the most outlandish. Jean Louis always has to make a statement."

"I don't see why we don't just haul him in for questioning. Hey, Jean Louis, did you hit an old lady on the noggin?"

"If he is really who I think he is, Jean Louis would never break. Never. He's much too clever."

"He can't be that clever if you saw through him."

I gave a teasing smile. "Maybe I'm more clever than he is?"

"You're smart-dumb."

I pulled back. Hadn't I heard that recently? "What does that mean?"

"It means that there are people who have very high IQs, but do stupid things like involving the police in a harebrained scheme like this."

"It will work. You'll see." Patting his chest, I gave him an inquisitive look. "Have you lost more weight?"

"What do you think?"

"About what?"

"How do I look?"

"What are you . . . a teenage girl?"

"My daughter says I look ugly sexy."

"She does, does she? Well, daughters love their daddies."

"That does it. Get your coat and let's go."

"Don't get all huffy. You look good. Your daughter's right."

Goetz would not be placated. "Come on. Let's get this over with."

Twittering, I gathered my coat.

"You can be such an old biddy, Josiah."

"Now you know how it feels to be played with," I shot back. It was obvious that I was still angry over how I had been treated in the death of Richard Pidgeon.

"Are you going to forgive me? Ever?"

"Maybe if you killed for me."

Goetz grabbed, pulling me toward the front door.

"And maybe if you quit handling me like a sack of potatoes."

"You know, I'm beginning to see why O'nan wanted to shoot you. I want to shoot you myself sometimes."

"Goetz, shut up."

"You shut up."

"*You* shut up."

Goetz started to reply and then thought better of it. Constantly upbraiding Josiah was not going to get her in his bed. He was going to have to come up with a better strategy.

Thinking I had won the battle of the wills, I remained quiet on the trip to the Big House. I didn't understand why Goetz was quiet too. Not then.

But he was busy planning.

38

Jean Louis was a little overwhelmed. What was supposed to be a little friendly cocktail gathering had turned into a full-blown costume ball. He only assented after June had promised that he would make his plane in plenty of time. In fact, all of his treasured paintings had been packed and sent ahead.

Lady Elsmere stood beside him in the reception line greeting the aristocracy of Bluegrass life . . . the horse people, artists, and politicians. A movie star sprinkled here and there along with TV people.

Jean Louis glanced at June, hoping that she was getting as tired as he was, but she was smiling and air kissing everyone. She seemed to be having a hell of a time. He just wanted to sit down.

"Hello."

Jean Louis looked to where the sultry hello had sounded. Before him stood a ravishing creature with dark hair swept up with diamond pins, wearing a black satin dress with jeweled straps. She smelled of lavender.

"Madame X," he inhaled as he beheld this angel.

The woman smiled. "Ah, you recognized the dress. I had an exact copy made."

"*Madame X*. Virginie Gautreau painted by John Singer Sargent in 1884. It caused a scandal due to its sexual nature."

"How could a portrait of a woman in a black dress standing by a table in front of a drab brown background cause a scandal?" smiled the woman.

"Because it was originally painted like this," replied Jean Louis, reaching over and slipping the strap off her right shoulder so that it fell on the upper arm. Jean Louis stepped back and gazed at the vision. "Breathtaking. Simply breathtaking. You are truly Madame Gautreau. Madame X."

"Oh, darling," gushed Lady Elsmere. "You made it."

"I wouldn't have missed this for the world. I just flew in from London."

"Asa Reynolds, may I present Jean Louis to you."

Jean Louis twitched a little upon learning the name, but he recovered quickly. Taking Asa's hand, he lightly kissed it. "Enchanté. You are the daughter of . . . "

"That's right," interrupted Asa, her dark eyes glittering in the candlelight. "Josiah Reynolds is my mother."

"I see only a faint resemblance."

"I take after my father."

"I see. Perhaps we can share a few moments later on. Your choice of painting interests me."

Asa beamed a bright smile in his direction. "I would love to talk with you, Jean Louis."

"Darling, you can talk later," interrupted Lady Elsmere, "but move along for now. You're holding up the reception line."

Asa laughed and glided into the hallway, grabbing a glass of champagne from a waiter on the way to the ballroom.

Many heads turned and stared. Some clapped when they recognized whom she was impersonating.

Asa nodded, acknowledging their admiration. Along the way, she looked for her mother and Detective Goetz.

While Mrs. Astor could only accommodate four hundred of New York's bluebloods in her ballroom, Lady Elsmere's ballroom wasn't designed for more than one hundred. It was already becoming a tight squeeze.

Asa found a quiet space in a corner of the candlelit room and scanned for her mother. She saw her on the other side dancing with Detective Goetz . . . and they were dancing very close. Too close, really.

Asa sighed. Maybe something was going on with her mother and Detective Goetz. That would take the sting out of telling her that Jake had remarried his ex-wife. But

Asa still hadn't decided if she was going to tell her mother. Asa knew that Josiah had really loved Jake. Maybe she should just stay mum on the subject.

Asa didn't get much time to reflect as a man dressed as a rakish cavalier bowed before her.

Asa curtsied and held out one hand. "My lord."

The man gently took her hand and led her out onto the dance floor. "You are Madame X. Who am I?" asked the dashing young man as he twirled Asa.

"You are my Lord and Liege, Charles II painted as a young man by Sir Peter Lely."

"Perfect. Brains as well as beauty."

"See that couple over there?"

Charles II looked to where Asa nodded. "Yes?"

"Take me over there. I want to talk with that woman."

"Your wish is my command," he quipped as he waltzed Asa in the direction of her mother.

Asa had to admit that Charles II was a very good dancer.

39

"Do you have to dance so close? This is supposed to be a waltz. You're doing a foxtrot."

"For once, will you let me take the lead?" complained Goetz.

Suddenly the waltz ended and the band played *All Of Me.*

Goetz pulled me closer and put his cheek against mine as he paraded us around the dance floor. "*All of me, why not take all of me? Can't you see that I'm no good without you,*" whispered Goetz.

"*Take my lips. I want to lose them. Take my arms. I'll never use them,*" I joined in.

Goetz mouthed in my ear, "*Your goodbye left me with eyes that cry. How can I go on, dear, without you?*"

I finished the song, *"You took the part that was once my heart, so why not take all of me?"*

I glanced up at Goetz. The intensity of his stare was too much. I looked away. I was not used to men looking at me so intently.

"Look at me, Josiah," he rumbled.

"I can't."

"Why not?"

"I'm afraid that I'll lose myself. I can't afford another mistake." I tried pushing him away, but Goetz's grip was firm. That man was strong.

He rested his cheek against my hair. "Don't be afraid. I won't hurt you. I'll never hurt you."

"You'll try to change me. Control me."

"Never."

I finally pushed out of his grip. "I don't ever want to love again. It hurts too much."

"I'm not that son-of-a-bitch Brannon."

"That's just it. Brannon was a wonderful man. We had many happy years, but his betrayal just about did me in. You might be a wonderful man too, but in the end, you'll betray me somehow. I just know it."

Goetz started toward me.

"Don't. Just don't," I cried as I fled the ballroom.

40

"Mommy, what are you doing in here? I followed you from the ballroom."

"Oh Asa, you made it!" I tilted my cheek for a kiss. "I came in here to hide."

We were in one of the unused guestrooms. I was sitting on the bed trying to figure out why Goetz frightened me so.

"Did the good Detective upset you? Why does that man always look like an unmade bed?" Asa added as an afterthought.

"I think it's because he looks like a Shar Pei." We both smiled at the thought of Goetz looking like a wrinkled dog.

"You didn't answer my question. Did he upset you?"

"Not really. It's just at times like this I wish your father were here . . . or Jake. I miss Jake, I guess."

Asa frowned. "Since you brought him up, there's something I've been meaning to tell you."

I held up my hand. "Please don't. I know he's not coming back. I don't need to know anything else. Okay?"

Asa sat on the bed and put her arms around me. "Sure, Mom. It can wait."

Asa smelled like lavender basking under warm sunshine.

"Is everything ready?"

"Everyone has been put in place," assured Asa. "All he has to do is go after the bait."

"And if he doesn't?"

"Then there is very little that can be done at this point."

I started to speak, but a gong sounded. Asa and I went out into the hallway where there was quite a bit of commotion.

We followed the crowd upstairs and peered over the ornate banister where Jean Louis and Lady Elsmere were enacting Jacques-Louis David's 1804 masterpiece *The Coronation of Napoleon* where he was placing a crown upon Josephine's head as Empress of the French Empire.

Jean Louis was dressed as a noble Roman wearing a golden olive wreath on his noble brow and white toga while sporting a red velvet robe embroidered with golden honeybees, exactly as Napoleon was attired in the painting.

Below him on the steps knelt Lady Elsmere in an exact replica of the regalia Josephine wore.

Behind her stood two of her oldest friends holding up the train of her enormous red robe.

In real life, the two women holding up Josephine's train were Napoleon's sisters who at the moment of kneeling tried to cause Josephine to fall by tugging on the train, thus embarrassing her in front of the European court that had come to witness the coronation.

However, Josephine managed to catch herself and kneeled with grace. You go, girl!

Everyone started clapping and yelling, "Bravo! Bravo!"

Jean Louis helped Lady Elsmere to her feet after which they bowed to the enthusiastic crowd.

Lady Elsmere quieted everyone. "I wish to thank you all for coming to see my new portrait by Jean Louis. Jean Louis, I wish to thank you for breathing new life into me. I am sorry to see my friend leave us tonight, but enough said. I hate long goodbyes. Everyone—enjoy yourselves."

As the crowd dispersed, Goetz made his way up the grand staircase to us.

"Hello Asa. You look very becoming tonight."

"Thank you, Detective Goetz."

"Come on, Josiah. This is your ballgame. No time to get cold feet."

"Are you going to quit trying to corral me?"

"Yeah. I'm going to let you chase me from here on out."

"As if I ever would."

Asa tilted her head listening to her mother and the Detective banter, but kept her thoughts to herself. "I'll get the smarmy Jean Louis myself," said Asa. "Shouldn't be too hard. Make sure that painting is gone."

"Let's do it," I pronounced. Leaning over the balcony, I caught Liam's eye as he was giving last-minute instructions to servants for the midnight buffet.

He nodded and very deftly walked past the John Henry Rouson painting and lifted it off the wall without attracting any undue attention. Like the true thief that Liam was, he walked away with the painting by his side and out of the room.

What was astonishing is that no one seemed to notice.

41

"Now, it is time for me to go into action," remarked Asa. Starting down the staircase, she looked for Charles II, turning down many offers to dance.

Finally wandering into the ballroom, she saw him dancing with a woman dressed as Ophelia as painted by Sir John Everett Millais. She could see that Charles II was having a hard time competing with Ophelia's large bouquet of flowers, which kept getting caught under his rather large nose.

Seeing Asa wave to him, Charles II rolled his eyes in dismay and promptly danced Ophelia over to a corner where he dumped her after thanking her for a lovely samba.

"I didn't mean to break up a meaningful relationship," quipped Asa after Charles II sashayed over to her.

"All Ophelias are bores and definitely in need of Prozac."

"I need your help."

Charles II's eyes lighted up. "Great. Who do I have to kill?"

"See that fat little man over there?"

"You mean the guest of honor, Jean Louis?"

"I want you to flaunt me right under his nose."

"And then."

"Turn me over to him when he cuts in."

"Very sure of your charms, aren't you?"

"You came when I waggled my finger."

Charles II smiled. "Touché, but I'm an easy touch. Desperate for female contact."

"So is he."

"Well, let's do the dirty deed," crooned Charles II as he whisked Asa around the dance floor to where Jean Louis was talking to admirers.

Immediately Jean Louis saw Asa out of the corner of his eye. "Excuse me please, but I must dance with this rare Kentucky flower before I leave tonight," he said to his little group before bowing.

Quickly he stepped onto the dance floor and tapped Charles II on the shoulder.

"So sorry to cut in, but Madame X promised me this dance." He stared at Asa as though daring her to call him a liar.

"He's so right. I'm sorry, but I did promise Jean Louis this dance," Asa said.

"Truly my loss," replied Charles II as he turned Asa over to the diminutive Jean Louis.

"I'm all yours," cooed Asa.

"If only I had more time," rhapsodized Jean Louis staring at Asa's décolletage. "I would love to paint you, maybe as an odalisque."

"That has been so done. Can't you think of something more original?"

"But a woman such as yourself needs to be adored, needs to be worshipped."

"I feel as though I'm being worshipped enough right now. Do you mind removing your hand from my derrière?"

Jean Louis gave Asa a sheepish grin before dipping her.

"Didn't expect that," groused Asa as she righted herself. This guy was a regular octopus. "Let's go out into the hall. It's so crowded and hot in here."

"Not at all, Cherie," Jean Louis said as he whisked her into the hallway.

There stood people gathering at the buffet table. Most were going into the dining room with their full plates while some gathered in the breakfast room.

A few couples were dancing in the grand entryway. Asa and Jean Louis joined them.

Jean Louis bantered on about his next portrait assignment until he stopped dead in his tracks. "The painting is gone," he ranted.

"What?"

"The John Henry Rouson painting is gone! The one I gave to Lady Elsmere. It's not here."

Asa turned and stared at the blank wall. "I think I heard Lady Elsmere say that she was donating it to the Headley-Whitney Museum for an equestrian art show. She sent it out to be cleaned and appraised."

Jean Louis gaped at Asa in wide surprise. "But that was not the stipulation of the gift. She was never to remove the painting and it was never to be cleaned. You must excuse me but I need to check on my luggage. I am leaving in just a few hours."

"But we were having such a good time."

"Do you know where the painting is now?"

"It's probably in Charles' office. He runs this place but he is on vacation."

"I know where that office is. It's on the other side of the house."

"Is there a problem with the painting?"

Jean Louis took out a perfumed handkerchief and mopped his sweating upper lip. "Everything is wonderful. Thank you for a lovely dance, Madame X."

Asa nodded and watched the little fat man rush up the grand staircase. "That's really a shame," said Asa, pouting to no one in particular. "He is such a good dancer. What a waste."

42

Much to Lady Elsmere's chagrin, Jean Louis didn't even say goodbye. It was assumed that he had called a cab and left during the party.

At least that's what Lady Elsmere assumed.

Everyone else knew differently.

43

Jean Louis knew his way around the Big House. He had hidden and waited until the last guest left at 2:15 a.m. and Liam had turned out the lights at 3:30 a.m.

He had to hurry. He knew that the horse staff started to arrive at 4:30 a.m., but he should be long gone before then. Of course, he would have been halfway to Europe by now if that stupid woman hadn't loaned out that painting he had given her. Thank goodness he had stumbled upon the fact it was going to have a cleaning. That just could not happen.

He quickly went to Charles' office and unlocked the door with a duplicate key he had made. Jean Louis had had duplicates made of all the keys to the estate. How else could he have gotten into June's estate checkbook and lifted several checks from the back? Nothing would be noticed until the checks were cashed and still the crime would not be tied to him. Maybe some suspicions, but no proof.

If a former benefactor caused a fuss about checks missing from a checkbook or an article of some importance missing from its nook, Jean Louis had already discovered something about the benefactor. Usually something naughty that the benefactor did not wish to be known to the world. That stopped all accusations.

But Jean Louis didn't have anything over the Lady Elsmere. Years ago, an affair between the mistress and the butler would have caused a scandal, but he knew June well enough to know that she would relish the notoriety.

Sometimes Jean Louis pined for the good old days when scandal was something juicy a grifter could really sink his teeth into.

Focus, thought Jean Louis. *Get that painting and get out.* He pointed the flashlight about until he flashed behind the desk. Not expecting to see a person, he cried out while dropping the flashlight.

44

The office suddenly flooded with light as a person sitting in the chair behind the desk flipped on the desk lamp.

Much to Jean Louis' chagrin, there sat Asa Reynolds holding the John Henry Rouson painting.

"Looking for this?" she taunted.

45

Gone was the black satin dress with jeweled straps. Asa was now wearing a black duster with evil looking black boots that came up mid-calf. Her hair was swept up in a French braid.

"You frightened me," complained Jean Louis. "Almost gave me a heart attack."

"Then maybe you shouldn't go sneaking around people's houses in the wee hours of the morning."

"I forgot something."

Asa laughed. "Yes, I know. You forgot this." She jiggled the painting.

"Don't do that, please."

"Why not, Jean Louis? I admit it is a handsome painting of some horses, worth some serious money, but not a great fortune."

"You don't know what you've got there."

"Maybe I do."

Jean Louis snorted. It sounded girlish. "Give me the painting, Asa, and I will cut you in."

"How about I cut this?" Asa flashed a switchblade toward the painting.

Jean Louis screamed, "Mon dieu, don't damage that painting! It's priceless!"

"What's the matter, Jean Louis?"

"If you harm that painting, I'll kill you. I swear I will!"

"No you won't. Violence is not your style. Oh, I admit you've been a bad boy most of your life, but hurting people physically . . . not you. You like to cheat, steal, con, extort, blackmail, and threaten your victims, but you've never gone beyond that. Maybe your daddy did."

"My papa's dead. Has been since the War."

"Not really. He died years after World War II."

"My father was a farmer who died in the Résistance," insisted Jean Louis, inching toward the door.

Your father was a German named Albert Boehmer, who was a member of the Kunstschutz. You know what the Kunstschutz was, don't you? A Nazi military unit specially formed to confiscate art and precious artifacts. And since Albert Boehmer was a close relative of Bernard Boehmer, a Nazi collaborator . . . the fix was in."

"I don't know what you are talking about. Fairytales. Rumors. Lies."

"Your great-uncle Bernard Boehmer, along with

Hildebrand Gurlitt, Ferdinand Moeller, and Karl
Buchholz were commissioned by Adolph Hitler and his
right-hand man Goering to sell sixteen thousand pieces
of 'decadent art' removed from German museums in
1937-38 to help fund the war effort. What was not sold
was to be burned and some of it was, but a great deal of it
was confiscated by those I mentioned who recognized
the paintings as great art and very valuable regardless of
the Nazi decrees that the art was garbage.

"The paintings were hidden, disguised, and passed
secretly down through their families . . . like your family."

"That's ancient history. Why keep the paintings a
secret now?" Jean Louis fumed.

"Because the museums might want their paintings
back . . . or the Jewish . . . or Gentile families from whom
the paintings were stolen. There would be lawsuits and
perhaps imprisonment. Who knows what the World
Court might decide? What I do know is that these
paintings don't belong to descendants of Gurlitt or
Moeller or Boehmer."

"Perhaps what you say is true, but where are these
stolen paintings, eh? I see nothing but a John Henry
Rouson that you are holding. It was painted long after
World War II."

"That's where I must congratulate you, Jean Louis.
It's *The Purloined Letter.*"

"De quoi parlez-vous?"

"A short story by Edgar Allen Poe where an
important document is hidden in plain sight."

"I don't understand."

"Stolen artwork hiding in plain sight, but you made some mistakes. We both know how paintings are insured. The backs of the paintings are photographed as well as the sides of the canvas. That's why most of your collection has the sides cut off and new canvas sewn on.

"That's what really gave you away. You never in your life dreamed that a guard from a famous museum would happen to be curious about new frames or sewn canvas on supposedly minor classics. He must have pulled one painting from its frame during the Valentine party and seen the new canvas sides. Dead giveaway.

"And I see in the bottom left-hand corner of this painting, a small scratch. My bet is that Mr. Bailey thought this painting might be a fake and deliberately scratched it. Maybe he thought it might have been a painting stolen from the Isabella Stewart Gardner Museum."

"That imbecile. I walked in on him taking a fork and scratching my beautiful painting."

"And Terry found that there was paint underneath."

"He began writing in a notebook. He accused me of defrauding Lady Elsmere and that I had given her a fake. Ah, if he had only known."

"What's underneath this Rouson, Jean Louis? I know the real John Henry Rouson painting is in a private collection."

"One of the most important paintings in the world. A Monet!"

One of Asa's eyebrows arched. She was not expecting this. "So you forge a minor masterpiece over a priceless masterpiece and give it to a patron for what reason?"

"I can't go about the world with these paintings. I paint over them and give them a safe place to hide, and then collect them when I want. I either steal them back or encourage the new owner to give them to me. I have keys to all the houses where I store my babies."

"Why not put them in a large safe deposit box in a bank?"

"How long do you think it would take other art collectors to know that an important art collection was in a bank vault and for that bank to be robbed or an employee to be bribed? The art world is very small. Non. Non. Must always be on the go and hide my babies where no one would think to look."

"Seems awfully complicated to me, but then it's part of the game. You like the extortion, the blackmailing, the stealing. When you want money, you tell the 'owner' what the true secret of the painting is and that you will call Interpol on them for having a stolen painting, or will expose some dark secret if they don't give you money."

"You make me sound horrible. I'm just trying to make a living."

"Let's get back to Terry. Did you kill him?"

"I saw his little black notebook and the scratch marks on the Rouson. I knew he was suspicious of something. Then I found out who he was and that he had been a guard at the Isabella Stewart Gardner Museum. He probably thought the painting was from the robbery.

"I went to see him. To frighten him a little. That's all."

"Mother had his dog tested. He tested positive for cyanide poisoning," lied Asa, trying to trap Jean Louis.

"I must confess that I went there with the intention of doing away with him, but I couldn't. Like you said, I'm not a violent person, but on the way out I poured the cyanide in the driveway. The dog must have come behind me and licked some of it."

"So you had nothing to do directly with the murder of Terrence Bailey?"

"He was murdered? I thought he died of a heart attack."

"Probably brought on from stress by you."

"Likely as that is, causing stress is not punishable or one spouse in all married couples would be cited for murder."

"What about Mavis Bailey?"

"What about her?"

"Did you try to kill her?"

"Again . . . I went looking for that little black notebook. She woke up and discovered me, so I had to give her a little tap on the head."

"Like you gave my mother a little tap on the head?"

Jean Louis shrugged. "Madame X, I have enjoyed our little chat, but I must be leaving now and with that painting since you now know what it is. I'm afraid I can't leave it behind."

"I'm afraid I must insist that you stay."

Jean Louis pulled a gun out from his coat. "I know I said I was not a violent man, but you are pushing me to be one. Now please hand over the painting and I will be on my way. If you insist on interfering with me, I will have no choice but to shoot you. Not personal, you understand."

"You insist?"

"I do."

Asa leaned over the desk and handed the painting to Jean Louis.

"Your phone on the floor, please."

Asa threw down her cell phone.

Jean Louis motioned with the gun. "Now we are going to take a little walk to the freezer. If you keep moving in place, you will be found before you freeze."

Asa got up slowly and moved past Jean Louis out the door with her hands held up.

Smug, Jean Louis followed her out the door. As soon as he walked out into the hallway, he felt a gun barrel at his temple and heard the click of a revolver.

46

"Give me a reason to shoot," groused Goetz.

Asa swirled around and grabbed the gun from a startled Jean Louis.

"This is not possible," complained Jean Louis. "You are after the wrong person. This woman," he pointed at Asa, "was trying to steal Lady Elsmere's painting. I was only trying to stop her."

"Nice try, but no cigar," commented Goetz as he pushed Jean Louis down the corridor.

"I am a French citizen. I have diplomatic immunity. You can not arrest me."

"Shut up," demanded Goetz, "or I'm gonna make you shut up."

"American police brutality," complained Jean Louis. "You heard it," he said to Asa. "You are my witness that this gorilla threatened me."

"I didn't hear him say anything," replied Asa. "I just hear you flapping your gums."

Goetz pushed Jean Louis into the kitchen where waited two police officers. "These nice men are going to take you down to the police station where a nice woman from Interpol is waiting to talk to you."

Jean Louis paled and then spat at Goetz. "They will learn nothing. You have no evidence. Nothing."

Asa stepped in front of Jean Louis. "That's not exactly true. You are misguided if you think that your paintings were loaded on a plane and flown out of the country.

"We got a warrant and they are at the Bluegrass Airport being gone over with OCT. You know what that is, I'm sure. Optical Coherence Tomography. They are going to see what's really underneath all that paint."

"You can't do that!" shouted Jean Louis. "Those paintings are mine!"

Asa smiled. "Dear boy, you know as well as I that if those are paintings looted by the Kunstschutz, you have no more right to them than the Man in the Moon. Admit it. You have simply lost."

Jean Louis' shoulders slumped and he gave Asa a mournful look as a police officer slapped handcuffs on him. "Madame X. How could you spoil such a lovely evening?"

"Besides the theft of the paintings, I'm going to see if I can pin a murder charge on you for the Baileys. You killed them with your harassment, just as sure as if you stuck a knife in their guts," sneered Goetz.

"I protest most vehemently. I did not kill that old couple. I may have threatened the old man. I may have hit his wife on the head, but it was not intentional. That couple died of natural causes. I'm sure the autopsies will prove that."

Goetz stuck his face so close to Jean Louis that they were touching noses. "If you weren't the direct cause, then you aggravated the events that lead to their deaths. I'm going to get you on something relating to their demise," promised Goetz.

He shoved Jean Louis toward an officer. "Get this scum out of my sight. He makes me sick."

Asa and Goetz watched the police put Jean Louis in a police cruiser and start down the driveway.

Then they heard clucking in the grand hallway and went to check on it.

Watching out a second floor window in their nightclothes stood Bess, Lady Elsmere, and Liam whispering to each other.

"You can come down now," yelled Asa. "The show is over."

"We did just as you said, Asa," blurted Lady Elsmere. "We stayed in my bedroom and didn't come out until we heard the police siren, but we are dying to know what happened."

"Go to bed now and I'll tell you later this morning. We're going to join Mother at the airport. She is assisting with the OCT on the paintings."

"Shoot, I could drop dead any time," groused Lady Elsmere. "I need to know now."

"Miss June, she's right. We are all very tired. I'll stay with you. You'll see. There is another day in store for you," comforted Bess.

Lady Elsmere gave a sweet smile. "I'd rather have Liam stay with me."

Liam's eyes flickered for a brief instant before he mumbled, "It would be my great pleasure to stay with you, Lady Elsmere."

Asa and Goetz looked at each other, but didn't comment. They didn't want to know and both excused themselves as fast as possible.

47

June and I sat glumly on a wooden bench in the church waiting for the funeral to begin.

"I should have done more," I recounted. "I didn't act fast enough."

"Who thought that pudgy little man could be so dangerous?" comforted June, who felt somewhat guilty herself. "After all, he was in the Bluegrass on my behalf. I had no idea that he was such a con artist. None."

"What did you do with his portrait?"

"I put it up in the attic. I hope like in Oscar Wilde's story, *Dorian Gray*, the portrait will take on my sins."

"That's a shame. It was a nice portrait," I fibbed.

"Do you think she will kick us out?" asked June, looking at Mavis' daughter glaring at us.

"I hope not. After all, I did go to her mother's rescue when she called, and solved her father's death."

"Do you think Jean Louis killed him?"

"The autopsy showed death caused by a heart attack. I think seeing Mavis' mother is what did the trick. Terry died of fright seeing a ghost."

"What do you mean, Josiah?"

"Terry was too savvy a guy to be frightened of Jean Louis. He knew a thug when he saw one. He could have just called the police with his suspicions if he was afraid.

"I think he was enjoying himself trying to solve whether the Rouson painting was legit or not. After all, if he could have solved the Gardner theft, he would have been a national hero. He didn't understand that the Rouson painting was part of something more sinister."

"So what you are saying is that maybe the heart attack was caused by seeing Mavis' mother."

"Uhmmm, that's what I just said," I replied, giving Lady Elsmere an odd glance. "Or maybe Mavis' mother came because she knew of the impending heart attack. I just think it was Terry's time to go, that's all."

"Uh oh, here she comes," warned June.

I tried to look sincere and humble, both of which were difficult for me.

"Hello, June. Hello, Josiah," said Mavis' daughter, tight-lipped. "Thank you for coming."

"Your mother was very nice to me, especially after my husband passed away. Of course I would want to be here," I replied.

"Can you tell me what happened to that dreadful man?" asked the daughter.

June winced. "My dear, I am so sorry. I had no idea what kind of man Jean Louis really was. He was an internationally known portrait artist. Everyone hired him."

"Silly vain women with too much money hired him, you mean," shot back Mavis' daughter.

June blinked. She was not used to people insulting her . . . except for me . . . and didn't know how to respond.

I cut in. After all, the daughter was mourning the loss of both parents in a short time. She had the right to cuss out people . . . for a while at least. "Jean Louis is still in custody. There was nothing in your mother's autopsy to try him for murder, but he is going to court for aggravated assault and then he will be tried overseas for various issues like theft of checks, blackmail, and possession of stolen goods."

"I hope he goes to jail for a long time," uttered the daughter.

"I'm sure Jean Louis won't see the light of day for a very long time," I concurred.

"That makes me feel better," the daughter replied. She glanced at her mother's coffin. "Much better."

"And I think you should realize that your father was on to him, and if not for that, those stolen paintings would never have been recovered. Terry is a bonafide hero," I said.

For the first time, the daughter smiled. "Thank you for saying that, Josiah. I would like my dad to get the recognition that was due him."

"I think if you turn around you will see a reporter from the *Herald Leader* snooping. Maybe you should tell your dad's story to him?"

Beaming, the daughter turned and rushed to the reporter who was taking quotes from anyone who would talk to him about the Baileys.

"Did you call the *Herald Leader*?" I asked June.

"And the *Louisville Courier Journal*. This is front-page news. In fact, there is a photographer in my home right now taking photos of my portrait painted by Jean Louis."

"The one that is stored in the attic?"

"Well, maybe it hasn't been put in the attic as of yet, but it will be . . . after everyone has seen it."

I chuckled. "Don't you have any shame?"

"I'm too old to have shame. It works out all right for everyone."

I nodded toward Mavis lying in a coffin. "Didn't work out right for her."

"I can't do anything about that, but I can try to see that her daughter gets some of the reward money for those missing paintings. Might even get a movie made about it. It has everything . . . suspense, crime, danger, sex . . ."

"Where does sex come into this?"

"My relationship with Liam, of course."

I coughed and looked around to see if anyone had overheard us. "You know he could sue you for sexual harassment," I whispered.

"I'm thinking of marrying him."

"WHAT!!!" I shouted.

"Oh, don't be so shocked. It will be a bit of fun for me. All the attention of a wedding."

"Surely you're not going to ask for wedding gifts?"

"Why not?"

"If you marry Liam, you won't be Lady Elsmere anymore."

"I won't?"

"I don't think so, but I'm not an expert on British peerage."

"Then I'll adopt him."

I stood up. I could tell my cheeks were red from embarrassment. "I'm not going to listen to any more of this insane conversation. If you adopt him, then you will have to stop having . . . you-know-what with him."

"Who made that silly rule?"

"Really, June. Are you going daft?"

June smiled.

"You evil old woman. You were just having a go at me."

"It's so easy, Josiah, to get your dander up and you're such a prude. Who would have thought it of you? Are you being prudish with Detective Goetz?"

"Why bring his name up?"

"Because he has been looking at you lately like a lovesick puppy, and the fact you both danced so close at the ball?"

"You are imagining things."

"Am I? Good morning, Detective Goetz."

I swung around in my seat. There hovering over us was, indeed, the good detective. I just hoped he hadn't heard any of June's babble.

"What are you doing here?"

"Thought I would pay my respects and tell Mrs. Bailey's daughter about Jean Louis."

"I've already done that."

"Would you like me to tell you about *your* daughter, Mrs. Reynolds?"

"My daughter? She's still at the airport helping to catalogue the paintings."

"Nope. She is on a plane to New York and then on to London. Asa tried calling you but your cell phone was off."

"That little turd!" I uttered, and then looked around to see if anyone had heard me. "Of course my phone is off. I'm at a funeral."

"She wanted me to tell you she had gone and that she would call you when she landed."

"Thank you for coming to tell me. I can't keep track of that girl."

Goetz nodded and moved on to talk with Mavis Bailey's daughter.

June started wheezing, "See, I told you. He's got love written all over him. Honey, hand me my flask. I've got the vapors."

I reached in her purse and discreetly handed the silver whiskey flask to June. As she was nursing her whiskey, I slumped against the bench that supported our tired selves. I felt deflated and used-up like thin butter on toast. I simply didn't have the courage to face my future and old age like June.

My daughter leaving took the wind out of my sails and if I was going to make it to dry land, I was simply going to have to change the direction of my ship.

"Excuse me, June," I said. "There is something I have to do." I went over to where Goetz was sitting and tapped him on the shoulder.

He swung around.

"Okay," I said.

"Okay, what?"

"You wear a suit. Bring candy and flowers. I'll be wearing a dress and high heels. No, I'll be wearing a dress and comfortable flip-flops. I can't wear high heels anymore."

Goetz looked amused. "And I'm wearing a suit . . . why?"

"To take me out on a proper date. Proper being the key word."

"Okay."

"Okay what?"

"Okay as in fine. I'll give you a call to ask you out for a proper date."

"I don't mean a beer hall or some cheesy restaurant."

"I get the idea."

"I want you to know that my days of falling in love are over."

"Does that mean no sex?"

"Ha-ha. Funny. We'll give this a whirl and see what happens. Game?"

"Game."

We shook hands and I returned to my seat next to Lady Elsmere.

She was smirking.

"What are you grinning about?"

"Nothing much, but Bess is going to owe me fifty dollars when I get home."

"What for?"

"She bet that you would never officially go out with Detective Goetz because of that gigantic grudge you have against him, but I know human nature. I said you would eventually succumb to Goetz wearing you down."

"You bet on me?"

"Oh, my dear, we bet on you all the time. You are fodder for our constant amusement. Now, don't get all huffy. You must admit you seem to have an amazing talent for getting into the thick of it. For two years there has been nothing but dead bodies around you."

"If that's true, aren't you worried?"

"Heavens no. You're one of the reasons I get up every morning. I just have to see what you are up to. Now, don't pout." June thought for a moment. "Would this little diamond ring on my right hand make you feel better, Josiah?"

"Most definitely. Hand it over. It will be salve to my wounded feelings like the Balm of Gilead." I put the ring on my finger and admired it.

Grinning like a cat that had drunk all the milk from the glass she had knocked off the table, June leaned over and whispered, "It's fake."

"Jumping Jehosaphat!"

Epilogue

I put down the *Herald Leader*. I had just read that Jean Louis was being extradited to Europe next week as the case against his involvement in Mavis' death was thrown out of court. There was no evidence that Mavis had died as a result of Jean Louis hitting her on the head. In fact, there was no evidence that Jean Louis had been in the house that night.

I certainly couldn't testify to the Grand Jury that he had been in the house the night Mavis was attacked. I may fib now and then, but I won't lie in a court of law or on the Bible. I just won't. I couldn't say I had actually seen Jean Louis that night.

So now he walks. I just hope that he gets a long prison sentence in Europe. Anyway, the news is out about him. Everyone knows what a scoundrel he is. Whether or not Jean Louis goes to prison, he is finished.

The paintings that have been recovered are being returned to their rightful owners.

As of this notation, the Isabella Stewart Gardner Museum theft has not been solved, but it will be in time. The paintings are probably in someone's private collection and sooner or later, some guest or employee will figure out what they are.

So you see, Bess' mother, Mrs. Dupuy, is right . . . the dark earth of Kentucky spits up the truth sooner or later.

This is Josiah Reynolds signing out . . . until the next time we meet.

BONUS CHAPTERS

From

<u>DEATH BY DERBY</u>
A JOSIAH REYNOLDS MYSTERY VIII

&
<u>LAST CHANCE MOTEL</u>
A ROMANCE NOVEL

DEATH BY DERBY

Prologue

Charlie Hoskins was a self-made man. He had been born into poverty in the Appalachian Mountains near where Jenny Wiley had been taken captive by the Indians in the eighteenth century. In fact, he was a descendant of hers.

Born poor as a church mouse, Charlie pursued his education with relentless single-mindedness, and once he received his BA from Murray State University, he pursued the obtaining of wealth with the same determination. He was relentless in his pursuit of money to the point that he was universally hated.

Oh, he was admired for his rags-to-riches story. He was admired for being a good businessman. But Charlie never learned tact and made lots of enemies in the process of realizing his dreams. He didn't care that in order to realize his goals, he had trampled on the dreams of others.

The reason most of us in the Bluegrass didn't care for bigger-than-life Charlie Hoskins was that he was a major developer in the area. Charlie seemed bent on buying every horse farm he could get his hands on and plowing them over with concrete for his many strip malls and housing developments. Many of his storefronts lay empty and barren, but that didn't seem to deter Charlie from building. He kept on and on destroying some of the most precious farmland in the United States in order to put up a parking lot.

Remind you of Joni Mitchell? If you don't know to whom I am referring, then you are not a child of the sixties . . . or a fan of good protest music.

But Charlie didn't care what people thought of him. Folks hadn't helped his family when they were down and out in the mountains, so he didn't care for their goodwill now.

But what Charlie did care about is that his Thoroughbred, Persian Blue, win the Kentucky Derby.

And next he cared about making a grand entrance into the Kentucky Derby in his hot air balloon on television. He was going to land his balloon right in the infield. Charlie was determined to be as well known as Donald Trump, his hero, and that entrance would be his introduction to the nation.

Charlie didn't seem to mind that Churchill Downs would forbid it. He hadn't asked them. He would just pay whatever fine he received and beg for forgiveness after he gave Churchill Downs a large donation for his reckless stunt.

Yes, Charlie was determined he was going to be a household name, no matter who he rubbed the wrong way.

1

I was just leaving Shaneika at Comanche's stall when I saw a hot air balloon drift overhead.

Shaneika and I watched it float past, wondering who was flying a hot air balloon so close to Churchill Downs on the day of the Derby. Then I saw Charlie Hoskins' name on the balloon.

"You've got to be kidding me," complained Shaneika.

We looked at each with disgust and then parted. I was going to get dressed in my finery, and of course my Derby hat, and join Lady Elsmere in her box at Churchill Downs. Mike and Shaneika would go to a different box to watch the Derby race, which was hours away but already TV crews were having pre-Derby shows.

I hadn't gotten several steps away when the balloon exploded and its basket plummeted to the ground. I quickly muttered a prayer, "Oh, God, please don't let anyone be hurt."

I turned and looked at Shaneika.

She stood rooted as she watched flames fall to the ground.

There was screaming from the track and horses were neighing from terror. People were running to safety, trying to dodge the flaming debris from the burning balloon.

I blinked several times trying to order my thoughts. Did I really just see a hot air balloon explode in the air? And if I had seen what I thought I had seen, had Charlie been in the balloon and fallen to his death?

I looked back at Shaneika. This was terrible and if Charlie had been in that balloon, it wouldn't be long before the police came to interrogate Shaneika.

Only last night, Shaneika and Charlie had had a terrible argument in front of witnesses at Lady Elsmere's Derby party. Shaneika had threatened to kill Charlie.

Shaneika stared back at me. I could tell she was thinking the same thing.

Shaneika might be in big, big trouble.

2

I have to go back to the beginning.

Charlie was not very popular with us . . . "us" being the Tates Creek clan–Lady Elsmere, Shaneika, Mike Connor, Velvet Maddox, Franklin, and me.

Shaneika had had run-ins with his staff concerning Comanche during Derby week. Charlie's boys were always standing too close to Comanche's stall or following Shaneika around the stables, deliberately bumping into her or whispering nasty things when they passed.

Even though Shaneika made a complaint against Charlie, nothing was done and the harassment continued. Shaneika, who was no shrinking violet, called for reinforcements, that being Mike Connor and myself.

"Charlie's people are trying to intimidate me," confided Shaneika.

I could see that Shaneika was unnerved by the harassment. She did not have her usual support with her. Her mother, Eunice Todd, was in Versailles taking care of Shaneika's son, Lincoln. They would not see Shaneika until she entered their box for the Derby race on Saturday.

"Charlie must think Comanche is a threat to Persian Blue," I replied, trying to put a good spin on her story. "I can't believe that the racing authorities did nothing."

Mike put his arm around Shaneika. "Don't worry, Shaneika. I put in a call to Velvet. She'll be here to calm Comanche. He's picking up on your nervousness. That's why Charlie is trying to unnerve you. Horses are sensitive to emotions."

I chimed in, "And we are here. Everything will be fine. It's only a couple of more days to the Derby. There's Lady Elsmere's party the night before. You can relax then and let your hair down a little."

"Josiah is right, Shaneika. I've pulled some men from Lady Elsmere's farm and they will guard Comanche around the clock from now on. You don't need to worry."

I could see the tenseness in Shaneika's face drain away. I wondered if it was due to the guards or the fact that Mike was going to be with her until the Derby was over.

I was happy that Mike was here for Shaneika. I

thought he was a good man and that his presence calmed the tightly coiled spring that was Shaneika.

Neither of us knew that Mike was going to be the reason Shaneika and Charlie would get into a fight at the party, and that it would escalate into such an ugly scene in front of so many people.

But when you threaten to kill someone and then they die from unnatural causes, you can expect the police to knock on your door.

And knock the police did.

Last Chance Motel
A Romance Novel

Eva gazed into the floor-length mirror and was pleased with her reflection. The black negligee she had recently purchased encased her trim body like a glove. Her auburn hair glimmered with highlights and her skin looked like butter cream. Even though she was forty, Eva looked younger and worked at it.

Hoping that her sexy look might heat up her husband, who seemed a little frost-bitten lately, she put on the finishing touch. Passion Fire Red lipstick!

Nine years ago she had met Dennis while helping his company remodel an old warehouse on the west side of Manhattan. Her boss had put Eva in charge of the cosmetic rehab of the warehouse while others dealt with structural issues. That was okay with Eva. Buying furniture and picking out paint colors was fun and she was given a huge budget with which to play.

It was at a briefing that Eva was introduced to Dennis, a junior executive at that time. He was to be the company's liaison with her.

There was instant chemistry and before long they were embroiled in a passionate affair, which spilled over into marriage two months after the project was completed.

Nine years. Eva shook her head in disbelief. Where had the time gone? Six of those years had been fantastic, but things started slipping three years ago.

It had begun when Eva and Dennis purchased an abandoned brownstone in Brooklyn near the Verrazano Bridge. They had been giddy when they first received the keys from the bank and began restoring the four-story brownstone, but things started taking a downward turn six months into the project.

To save money, Eva and Dennis decided to complete many of the cosmetic projects themselves. After working long hours at their firms, they would hurry home to the brownstone and work late into the night trying to tile the bathrooms or lay down bamboo floors or paint twelve foot ceilings. What started as fun became a strain both physically and mentally.

They began snapping at each other and it didn't take long to realize that they both had different visions for the brownstone, which created even more tension.

Eva wanted to restore the brownstone to its authentic former glory while Dennis wanted to gut and modernize it completely.

Dennis won.

When the brownstone was completed, Eva had to admit it was stunning, complete with all modern amenities. But to Eva, the brownstone was cold and void of any personality, but it was what Dennis liked. She disliked the cold paint colors he had chosen and the minimalist look of each room.

Eva realized that compromise was the cornerstone of marriage and wanted Dennis to be happy. That was very important to her. She could live with the renovation.

Now that the brownstone was finished, Eva wanted to heat up her faltering relationship with her husband and get it back on track.

Eva masked her irritation when Dennis finally got home . . . late as usual during the past seven months. Hearing the elevator rise to the master bedroom floor, Eva waited in the alcove trying to look sexy in her negligee.

The elevator reached the top and the door swung open. Dennis was going through the mail and barely looked up.

"Hello there, big boy," teased Eva.

Dennis looked up and froze when he saw Eva.

Eva noticed his hesitation and it threw her off her game. She suddenly felt foolish.

"What's up with you?" asked Dennis.

Eva, determined that the night be a success, smiled. "I thought we would celebrate your new promotion and the completion of the house. I have made a very nice dinner for us and then for dessert . . ."

"We celebrated last Saturday with our friends," retorted Dennis. He looked frustrated and a bit embarrassed.

"Yes, but I thought we could have a private celebration, just you and me," rejoined Eva.

Uh oh. This was not going as planned.

"Honey, I'm tired. I just want to eat and go to bed."

"Long day at the office?"

Dennis looked at the letters in his hand. His face was flushed. "Something like that."

"I have something that will make you feel better," chirped Eva. She was going to hit this out of the ballpark. Eva handed him two airline tickets.

"What's this?" Dennis asked, staring blankly at the tickets.

"I purchased two tickets to Miami for this weekend. The two of us on a getaway. No work. No house to think about. Just warm breezes and blue water. We can rent a boat and . . ."

"NO!"

"No?" echoed Eva. Her heart began to sink. Something was very wrong.

"This has got to end," Dennis said, cutting in, letting the mail fall to the floor. He looked at Eva as though he was looking through her. "I'm sorry I have let this go on for so long, but things have got to change."

Alarmed, Eva tried to hug Dennis but he pushed her away. Eva gasped. "What is it, Dennis? What's wrong? Are you ill?" She felt a numbing fear move up her spine.

"I'm sorry, Eva, but I'm not going anywhere with you. This is very hard to say but I . . . I want a divorce."

Eva felt like a bullet had passed through her. "What? For heaven's sake, why? We have everything. We worked so hard on this house. Why Dennis? Why?"

"I don't love you anymore. That's why."

2

"Mr. Reardon wants the brownstone," demanded Dennis' lawyer.

Eva and her attorney sat across the conference table. "Where is Dennis?" Eva asked. Turning to her lawyer, she questioned, "Shouldn't Dennis be here?"

"Mr. Reardon has given me instructions to act on his behalf and feels his presence is not necessary under the circumstances."

"What circumstances? Not seeing me?" Eva asked.

"Eva," cautioned her lawyer. "Let me handle this."

"What circumstances are you referring to?" Eva asked again.

"I believe that Mr. Reardon has expressed concern about you being abusive lately."

Eva snorted in derision.

"Many women become upset when asked for a divorce and given no reason. Mrs. Reardon has been a faithful and constant companion to Mr. Reardon. I think that under the circumstances most women would raise their voices and maybe even throw some objects. It's human nature."

"Mr. Reardon feared for his life."

"Oh, please," scoffed Eva. "Give me a break."

"If Mr. Reardon feared for his safety he should have called the police and filed a complaint. Since there is no complaint, let's move on, shall we. Alleging that Mrs. Reardon is a threat without proof is counter-productive to your client's requests."

"Demands," rebuffed Dennis' lawyer.

"What are they?" asked Eva's attorney, putting a pencil to a legal pad.

"Quite simply, Mr. Reardon wants the brownstone." Dennis' attorney raised his hand. "I have been authorized to offer eight hundred thousand for your half, Mrs. Reardon, plus half of all moneyed accounts that you share with Mr. Reardon. I think it is a very equitable division of assets."

"I don't understand why Dennis would want the brownstone. It's too large for one person. I thought we were going to sell it and divide the proceeds," remarked Eva.

"They think that they . . ." the lawyer stopped suddenly, looking aghast at his faux pas.

"They?" questioned Eva.

"I meant he," stated Dennis' lawyer.

"You said 'they'."

Shaken, Eva leaned back in her seat. "They. That explains a lot. It's the missing piece of the puzzle of why he left me." She began to sob quietly.

Her lawyer closed his notebook. "Tell Mr. Reardon that Mrs. Reardon wants 1.2 million plus half of all the other assets or we are going to drag this out indefinitely."

"Oh no, you can't do that," complained Dennis' attorney. "The house needs to be available by the next several months before the . . ."

Both Eva and her lawyer's mouth dropped open at the implication of the statement.

Eva began to wail out loud.

Her lawyer stood and helped Eva to her feet. "I assume that Mr. Reardon's new friend is pregnant then. He'll meet our demands or I'll tie up that brownstone for years."

"Oh God," whispered Eva, being led from the conference room. "He's got a new woman and they're going to have a baby in my house. My house! I painted every room! I installed the tile! I refinished the wood floors!" She yelled, "This just went from bad to the absolute worst. He told me he didn't want any children."

Eva grabbed a woman in the hallway. "He said he would love me forever."

"They all say that, dearie. But if they can afford it, they trade us in every ten years or so for a new model. Once the tits start to sag, it's over," replied the stranger in sympathy. "We've all been there. It's just your turn now."

"What happened to true love?" murmured Eva.

Her lawyer snickered. "Surely you don't believe in that crap, do you? Just get the money and run."

"But I do. I do believe in true love," blurted Eva and she cried this mantra all the way home, that night and for the next several days until her body became so dehydrated she couldn't cry anymore.

3

Three months later, Eva signed the divorce papers and slipped them in the stamped mailer as directed. Licking the flap, she closed the mailer with a large sigh. "Well, that's the end of that," she said.

She hurried downstairs so she could catch the mailman whose truck she saw from the window. She caught him coming up the stoop and handed him the mailer.

Giving her a startled look, the mailman grabbed the envelope and hustled down the steps.

"I'm not that bad," she groused, noticing his reluctance to stay and chat.

A mother pushing a stroller hurried by when the toddler saw Eva and started to cry.

"Oh, come on now," complained Eva. Defeated, she pulled back inside the brownstone and looked in the hall mirror. "Jeez." Eva tried to flatten messy hair that would give Medusa a run for her money. Her eyes were sunken, teeth were yellow and dirty, and her skin was sallow.

Her outfit was pajamas that had not left Eva's body for the past two weeks and were straining at the seams as her new diet consisted of chocolate ice cream . . . and then strawberry ice cream . . . and again chocolate ice cream. With chocolate syrup. For a dessert, she inhaled Reddi-wip from the can.

And she stank.

"I'm in some deep, deep doo-doo," lamented Eva looking in the mirror and repelled by what she saw. "You're made of better stuff than this. You're just forty. Only six months ago you were hot stuff." She pulled on her belly fat. "Crap. I'm middle-aged now. The bloom has faded."

She gave the mirror one last pathetic look. "I just can't stop living. This is just a bump in the road." She took another hard look at herself. "Oh, who am I kidding? This is a freakin' firestorm!"

Coming to the realization that she had to battle her depression, Eva climbed the staircase to the third floor. There she took a long shower, washed her hair, shaved her legs, and put on some clean underwear. Looking around the bedroom, she found a pair of clean flannel pj's and a tee shirt. To complete the outfit, she slipped on some beat-up flip-flops.

Hungry, she went to the kitchen but found nothing in the fridge to eat. Frustrated, she began looking for carryout menus when she spotted the airline tickets to Florida.

Eva bit her lip as tears clouded her eyes. "I'm not going to cry," she whispered. "All that is over. I'm going to buck up and get over this. I'm going to get a new life."

Staring at the plane tickets, Eva suddenly called her travel agent and ordered a new ticket to be waiting for her at the airport. Then Eva grabbed her coat and purse as she fled the brownstone.

Giving the brownstone one last look, Eva flipped the house key down a street grate.

Dennis would be surprised to discover that Eva had had the locks changed and she had just thrown the only front door key into the New York City sewer system.

Eva felt an immediate sense of relief.

Hailing a cab, she instructed the driver, "JFK please, and step on it."

4

It took only a few hours to fly to Miami.

Eva stepped outside the airport and greedily soaked in the sub-tropical heat. She hailed a cab and got in.

The cab driver didn't seem too happy after getting a good look.

Seeing that the cabbie was dubious, Eva threw a fifty dollar bill at him.

"Take me to the Fontainebleau Hotel, please," she requested. She had always wanted to stay at the Fontainebleau since it was the hotel used in the James Bond film, *Goldfinger.*

"Are you sure, lady? It costs a lot of money to stay there," he said, eyeing her pajama outfit.

Thankful that she was wearing sunglasses so the driver couldn't see how ridiculous she felt, Eva pulled her coat close about her. "Remember Howard Hughes wore pajamas during the day and he was the richest man in America."

"Really? Never heard of him," the driver replied as he pulled out into the traffic.

"Leonardo DiCaprio played him in a Martin Scorsese movie. You might have seen it."

"Oh yeah. He was that guy who peed in jars and kept them in his room." He glanced in the mirror at Eva.

"You don't do that, do ya lady?"

"Not lately."

"'Cause that is disgusting."

"I would have to agree. You don't have to keep looking back here. I'm not peeing on your seats."

The cabbie shook his head and muttered, "I get all kinds."

"What was that?"

"Nothing, ma'am. Be there soon. You've missed the rush hour."

Eva settled into the back seat and stared out the window.

Unlike New York with its cold gray shadows and dark alleys, Miami was flooded with brilliant sunlight that danced off glass skyscrapers. New York was a concrete jungle, but Miami was the Emerald City. Everywhere were vast expanses of deep turquoise water, white sails, expensive cars zooming here and there and sun-drenched mansions.

Suddenly it was too much for Eva. She felt overpowered by the immense glass city, which resembled a mirror. It made her feel raw inside, too exposed.

"Listen," she said throwing a hundred dollar bill into the front seat. "I've changed my mind. Get me out of here."

"Where you want to go?"

"I'm not sure. All this glass and sun. It's too hectic. I need something calmer."

"The Everglades?"

"God, no! The last thing I need is to encounter an alligator. I just got rid of one reptile in my life."

"Depends on what you're looking for. How about the Keys?"

That was a possibility. Things were slower in the Keys, weren't they? And she didn't know a soul in the Keys. Not a one.

"I just want to rest. Relax."

"Then Key Largo."

"Key Largo," murmured Eva, thinking of the Lauren Bacall and Humphrey Bogart movie. "Yes, take me there."

"Where in Key Largo?"

"Just a nice hotel."

"How nice?"

"A hotel with a nice pool. I like to swim."

"Motel okay?"

"No. I want a hotel. One that will have a concierge."

"You got more money?"

"YES! Just get me to Key Largo." Exhausted, Eva fell back against the seat. "Please, no more talk. Just drive."

Sulking, the driver changed lanes and made his way to Highway 1 heading for the Keys.

Two hours later, the driver stopped in front of an expensive chain hotel. "This okay, lady?"

Eva looked out the car window and nodded. "It will do for now." She paid the driver the exorbitant fare plus a two hundred dollar tip.

He no longer thought Eva was crazy but merely eccentric. Rich people were never crazy, just different. She would make a great story for his family over dinner. Eva motioned for the hotel valet to open the cab door and help with various packages.

She had stopped at a mall on the way and had purchased some casual outfits. As soon as she stepped out of the cab, the silky breezes of the Keys enveloped her.

Eva took a deep breath.

The salty air smelled like home.

She felt the pain in her broken heart dull a little.

Eva no longer felt that she was going to die.

Perhaps with a little luck she just might recover . . . even flourish.